MUTINY

ABOARD THE STARSHIP ICHTHUS

Brent Winzek
with C.J. Barrett

Space Cadets Studios

Winner of the Pencraft Summer 2025 Best Book Award
for Science Fiction.
Winner of the 2025 Living Now Book Awards
Bronze Medal for General Fiction

Cover Art by Monica Kay
Edited by Matthew Lapidus
with assistance from Caedon Venné

Based on a play of the same title by Brent Winzek
& inspired by characters in the
Space Cadets video series (2005 – 2009)

DEDICATION

To Krista; a loyal, loving sibling in both blood and spirit.

ACKNOWLEDGMENTS

This book would not be possible without the editorial eyes of cohorts Matthew Lapidus and Caedon Venné, or the expertise & enthusiasm of co-writer C.J. Barrett. My deepest gratitude and love to my wife, cover designer & artist Monica Kay; without you, I am just words on a page. A tip of the cap is due to the great American playwright Eugene O'Neill, whose dramatic piece *The Hairy Ape* first prompted this idea. Conceptual inspiration was also drawn from the novel *Douglas Adams's Starship Titanic* by Terry Jones. Furthermore, this story would not exist without the Komeopian aliens, first created for the *Space Cadets* video series in 2006 with heavy influence from performers Collin Lindberg & John Scott. Lastly, this story would not be back in the *Space Cadets* universe (where it belongs) without the ever-engaging notes and ideas of Space Cadets Radio co-writer & co-creator Jordan Stine, who also served as the test reader for this novelization of *Mutiny*. Cheers, dear friend, and thank you as always for the inspiration.

-From the desk of B. Winzek

REFERENCE

For the reader who prefers a deep dive into worldbuilding, be on the lookout for footnotes which provide historical context for the *Space Cadets* universe.

EPIGRAPH

If humans cannot see ourselves when we look at each other, how will we ever reconcile an encounter with beings who in no way reflect our own image?

-Author Brent Winzek

CONTENTS

FOREWORD

From the Desk of Telfera Galikor
August 11th, A.D. 2319

Enclosed is my first-hand account of perhaps the most traumatic experience in all my years as a travel journalist. I hope that posterity will forgive me for keeping these harsh truths of my survival experience a secret for all my waking years. We are only so strong, even in our most resilient moments, and I was not strong enough to bring these details to light while I was alive to feel the consequences.

If you are reading this, I have departed this life. Do not mourn for me; I truly lived, and through my work travels, I saw the known universe. My life was full, and perhaps selfishly, I kept my secrets about the *Starship Ichthus*. Now that I am free from the judgements of this world, I must set history's record straight about the mutiny aboard the *Starship Ichthus*…

1. FIRST IMPRESSIONS

July 6th, A.D. 2299
20:25 Interplanetary Standard Time

When I first laid eyes on the *Starship Ichthus*, a sickening unease rattled my intuition. At first, I suspected it was merely the Gothic designs of that monstrous ship towering above my little boarding ferry. So dizzying was its effect, that I felt wholly insignificant waiting in the starship's shadow. The vast engines, the towering funnels, the rows upon rows of piping which made it impossible to count the decks by their brightly lit windows. It reminded me of my first encounter with a battle cruiser; a gargantuan military vessel that slogged through space with all the grace of a bloated corpse.

My eyes traced the portholes of *Ichthus* as they stretched into the distance, converging and melting away, indistinguishable from the very stars themselves, which all around glittered their countless forgotten pasts.

The *Starship Ichthus* was, as advertised, 'larger than life.' Most things at the turn of the twenty-fourth century were. Back then, people desired a size that matched the grandeur of the ISF[1] itself. Even I was guilty of it, yearning for sunlight and wide-open spaces the more I was confronted with tiny rooms aboard long cruises.

The size of a ship like *Ichthus* could not be fully appreciated in a holograph or viewed in a periodical such as the aptly named *To the Stars*, for which I write. It was one thing to see such a starship scaled against the Celestial Palace in Cortallek[2] or the orbital naval yards of old Jupiter. But it was quite another thing to receive this colossus in the boarding station, trembling at the foot of its mighty, curving bow. It was, in fact, nothing short of stupefying: the most ambitious feat of interstellar engineering in the history of our modern

---

[1] Interplanetary Space Federation – The larger, wealthier of two interplanetary governments in the known universe. Originally known as the 'Clipto-Terran Alliance,' the ISF started as a war-time partnership between the planets Earth and Cliptorgia to combat the transgressions of a neighboring star-system, Candalos Prime. Because of this, the war against Candalos Prime is referred to as 'The War of Formation,' though it is also nicknamed 'The Great War.'

[2] The capital city of the Interplanetary Space Federation, Cortallek is both the birthplace and the current seat of Cliptorgian civilization. Built amidst a lush, forested bay, Cortallek is the perfect example of the harmonious balance between nature and technology that Cliptorgian tradition strives to maintain, incorporating four distinct ecosystems within its urban sprawl.

age. And my gut kept trying to tell me it was a disaster waiting to happen. Context clues may have gotten me farther if I weren't so used to tuning out my anxious mind.

I shook my thoughts loose as a frantic alert beeped repeatedly from someone's device. The skipper of my little boarding ferry, who was no more than a meter or two away from me at the steerage console, swatted desperately at his WristCom, quickly silencing the alarm. I couldn't help but notice the concern that wrinkled his brow as he read the alert message on his device's little screen.

Next, he pressed a button at the steerage console and his voice rang out over the cheap loudspeaker for all present company to hear.

"Attention, ladies and gents; looks like we're experiencing a slight technical delay. I've been instructed to hold here for another ten-to-fifteen minutes. Bear with us; we want to make your cruise as care-free as possible!"

As he spoke, our ferry shuddered. The skipper had killed the engines. I sighed. In my experience, the station wouldn't have boarded us so soon had they realized we'd be stuck waiting.

I noticed the string of luggage crates leading into the chasm of *Ichthus'* belly. More specifically, I fixated on a freight shuttle as it veered away from the ship's keel. The rear luggage crate it was towing nearly sideswiped another shuttle careening out of control away from the ship.

The struggling shuttle zipped underneath us, as if it were making a hasty getaway. In that moment, I distinctly saw the flash of metallic green wings tipped in bright orange as a small fighter arced away from Embarkation Station. I knew it had to be an ISF fighter. More likely, it was a decommissioned military fighter now reassigned to Orbital Guard. Only law enforcement vessels were permitted to use hazard orange accents to denote their vessels.

I leaned against the window, searching in the direction both little vessels had gone. Other passengers were starting to mumble about it, as well. Like me, several others had leaned forward, all but pressing their faces to the glass of our ferry's vast windowpanes.

"What's going on," a concerned old man muttered.

"That was an armed fighter," someone else divulged to a travel partner in hushed tones.

Another flash of orange wingtips zipped by, ducking back under our boarding ferry. Then, a subtle rumbling shockwave rippled through our vessel, causing most everyone to gasp, or grip a handrail, or both.

The skipper picked up the loudspeaker again, laughing nervously into it. "Attention passengers; it seems that, uh, Orbital Guard is running an unscheduled – but very routine – security drill. We apologize for any inconvenience."

His explanation only fanned the flames of impending passenger gossip.

With our scheduled boarding at twenty-three hundred hours, all of Embarkation Station had gone into night mode an hour prior. Overheads were powered down in favor of a gentle blue ambient glow. It made for an eerie backdrop to the crowd's gathering concern.

We were in orbit around Cliptorgia[3], held just outside the gravitational forces of my homeworld's thick band of rings. We were on the dark side of the planet, and I could barely discern that familiar ribbon of color caused by the rings in the swathe of starlight.

The skipper's steerage console dinged a gentle alert. He activated the Com. "Ferry Four-one-two, responding to your boarding request," he said formally.

The Com's tiny speaker buzzed, and a voice responded, seemingly from a faraway, empty room. "Yeah, bring 'er around to starboard. They want me to send you to Boarding Hatch Forty-nine."

"Will do," the skipper said. He clicked off his Com and grabbed the wheel at steerage. I could tell he'd been waiting to do that just by how eagerly his hands gripped the levers, his knuckles whitening. The skipper flipped those levers, and our boarding ferry shifted. An

---

[3] The second planet in the Cor system and capital of the Interplanetary Space Federation. Cliptorgia is shared by two intelligent species: the land-dwelling mammalian Cliptorgians and the aquatic amphibian Hulgarians. They strive to live in concert with the natural forces of their planet. To maintain their planet's natural balance with the needs of civilization, Cliptorgia's entire western hemisphere has been cordoned off as a nature preserve for over one thousand years.

alarm thonked, and the ferry shuddered as it detached from Embarkation Station. I had to steady myself on an overhead handrail. In the windows behind me, the boarding station drifted away, and our ferry settled into a holding position along the upper decks of the massive starship.

As we drew nearer the grandiose *Starship Ichthus*, the interior of our little boarding ferry sparkled in reflections dancing off the stately vessel's copper hull and green glass. The refracted light bounced into our ferry as if twinkling off the surface waters of some atomic alien ocean.

The viewports swept to the great ship's stern, and the starship's engines filled our windshield. They were magnificent… almost hypnotic when I stared too long, as I often did. Three large cylinders protruded from the starship's triangular stern. Two were situated slightly above the ship's gunnel, and the third was centered underneath them. Dozens of small thrusters dotted the stern around those three large burners. Although the burners were dark, the engines were priming. I could tell because the glow of all those thrusters flickered blue like the center of a flame, staring back at me like the many blinking eyes of some giant insect crouching in the blackness of space.

How enchanting, I marveled internally.

I shifted my weight from one leg to the other and found my arms crossed, pressing against my chest. It was then I first acknowledged it: the sudden unease bubbling up from my gut. It was a great anxiety, as though a shroud of doom lay over the voyage of the *Ichthus*. I don't know from whence it came or how long it had been incubating inside me, but it hatched and took hold of me in that instant.

The insect eyes of the starship's thrusters, magical though they first seemed, glared at me now. What was bright and hypnotizing grew angry, as if I could look past those dazzling embers of pre-flight burn and discern the shadowy crevices beyond. The thin veneer of glamour was cracking, revealing the darkness beneath. Something was hiding in that darkness, but what it was, I could not tell.

'Don't be so dramatic,' I heard my mother's unsolicited advice scold. It's exactly what she would've said if she were there with me, and I suspected she'd be right. I just hadn't had enough sleep; there was too much on my mind.

The feeling which had been so strong a second before now subsided, burying itself deep down where I could forget about it. My imagination did tend to get carried away when I ran on limited sleep. It made trusting my intuition a difficult venture.

The boarding ferry veered away from the engine's empty glowing eyes and traveled along the port side of the ship, raising at a diagonal as we no doubt approached our gangway. On the bottom quarter of the hull, spanning the length of *Ichthus*, rows of massive pipes protruded, running from the outer engine casings to the bow and upwards to the directional thrusters amidships. It gave the ship a rugged air, like some wild animal trapped in a livestock cage.

From inside those dark cage bars, liquid seemed to churn, and strange lights darted this way and that. I say strange because they didn't seem to behave as one expects mechanical lighting to. Rather, some drifted along like a leaf on the wind… while others struggled like small fish in a strong current. There was no rhyme or reason to it, from what I could tell.

I approached the skipper at the controls of our boarding ferry. "Excuse me," I said gently, "I don't think I've ever seen lights quite like that on a star-liner before. What are they?"

"Those?" He popped his cap up and scratched his head, as if he had to think about it. Then, he smiled and said confidently, "That, ma'am, is the lifeblood of the ship." He punctuated his statement with an amused little chuckle.

A succinct if not ambiguous answer.

But then, I wasn't in on the joke yet.

Our ferry pitched slowly upward, climbing to the top decks. Brightly lit cabins, spacious promenades, and elegantly designed bronze casements and tempered green glass slipped past the windshield. As the ferry commenced boarding procedures, the backdrop of infinitesimal stars was broken by three immense voids issuing from the Shuttle Deck: the exhaust funnels. More inexplicable uneasiness crept in as I beheld the many-faceted constructs. There was something peculiar about these towers of bronze metal. Demented church organs, they were, with nests of pipes and tubes huddled around their bases; some stuck straight up like lofty trees while others bent and flared away like grasping claws.

A loud clank and subtle shake announced that our ferry had made contact with an umbilicus connector. It jolted me away from my growing qualms.

"If you would make your way to the gangway door, we can get started boarding you all," announced the skipper.

Two aggressively eager old women scooted up to him first. After a brief exchange with the young skipper that left them squawking and shaking their heads, they both began digging through their handbags.

"And please, please have your boarding passes ready to show me," the skipper added, smiling patiently at the women. "They must be ready to scan as soon as you reach the other end of the umbilicus. Many of your fellow passengers are still waiting to embark. Thank you!"

So, bunched together like Raffe[4] for the slaughter, we inched forward step-by-step through the bulkhead door. Then, we crept into the darkness of the black, rubbery umbilicus laced with its intricate bronze framework.

---

[4] Girthy quadrupeds often compared to ornithischian dinosaurs of Terran prehistory. Native to the Outer Rim world of Hierrnaus, Raffe are kept as livestock, much like cattle on Earth. Unlike cattle, their rapidly decaying waste and modest dietary needs make these creatures far less taxing on an ecosystem… if you can forgive the smell.

2. DEPARTURE

"Your ticket, ma'am," the winded, red-faced steward gasped as I cleared the umbilicus. The sight of his red cheeks against his cream-white uniform was alarmingly colorful, particularly juxtaposed with the vast black tile he stood before in the main gangway. I had my ticket pulled up on my datapad, which I held out for him.

He scanned its code with his frequency-gun, barely examining the readout on his screen. A green light on his device blinked and a mechanical chirp squawked in confirmation.

"Welcome aboard," he strained. "Please stand off to the side here, and a porter will be along shortly."

Caught off-guard, I allowed him to herd me aside. I tried to mind my manners, smiled, and said, "Thank y-"

"Your ticket, sir." He was already on to the next passenger, interested only in serving his purpose. There was no need for actual social interaction with this one. That wasn't unheard of, but it certainly was uncommon aboard such grandiose cruises. I kept these thoughts to myself as I carried on into the reception hall.

"Oohs," and "Aahs," issued forth from the passengers filing in behind me. However, I was not terribly impressed with the interior. There was nothing wrong with it, per se, it was just... pedestrian for the foyer of a Terran starliner. All the typical accouterments were there: black and white checkered floor, elongated Monticello windows port and starboard, various potted plants, all highly exotic in their origins, and, of course, marble tile.

Ivy-festooned trellises were strewn along the walls. Crystal chandeliers dangled from the ceiling. There were always, inevitably, crystal chandeliers. As I said, nice, but perhaps a bit too 'classical.' It was, to be blunt, in need of some inspired design choices. I felt as if the ship's heavy gothic exterior had perhaps worried investors, and they over-corrected on the exterior with predictable influences. The materials used to make it, however, seemed top-of-the-line. The marble was real stone, the tile was real clay, and the wood was real timber, through and through. Any synthetics were so well disguised they eluded my detection.

Ambling to the nearest queue of passengers waiting for their bags, I stood behind a rather rotund woman in a deep burgundy dress, carrying a fluffy white hand warmer, and wearing one of the most ridiculously wide-brimmed hats I'd ever seen. It's no secret that Terran women love wearing their hats on formal occasions, especially when boarding a starliner, and many are very tasteful and well-crafted, but this – this looked like she was trying to win a contest. She must have seen me staring, for she turned to face me square on. Her beady eyes looked me up and down with an arched eyebrow before they continued to scrupulously inspect the room before her.

Her handwarmer wriggled, then whipped its head around and locked two nearly crossed eyes on me. It was a dog! The toy canine curled back the corners of its mouth, trying to bare teeth from under all its fluff. It yipped as it struggled to crawl up her arm after me.

"No," the woman scolded. "Hush! Reginald, no!" She glowered in my direction, then very intentionally turned her back to me completely. Although he had lost sight of me, I heard fluffy Reginald's low, sustained growls: a warning for me to stay back.

A minute or two passed.

The line edged forward.

Another minute…

What in the world was taking so long?

I became aware of a steady hum – waited for the familiar vibration of massive engines that would take hold next. Were they priming the engines already? That didn't seem right. There were still ferries flying into position along the cruiser's gangways.

Even though the woman and her little white sentinel were now well ahead of me, Reginald had spotted me again and growled and grumbled. A young

Cliptorgian girl in porter's attire was trying desperately to lift the woman's bulging steamer trunk onto a nearby luggage rack as Reginald yapped loudly in her face.

Come now, Reggie: play nice, I thought with a smirk.

Poor girl.

Though the critter's protestations drifted out of earshot, the thrumming persisted. It was clearer to me without the snarls of an overstimulated lapdog. The gasping gurgle churned my anxious chest to a boil.

Where was it coming from?

Certainly not from anything I could see.

It ceased for a moment before grumbling again.

Then it hit me; it was coming from the floor.

I looked down. Along the baseboards, I traced several bronze pipes to a strange cylindrical tank in a shadowy corner behind me. A clear glass door showcased bubbling water that glowed toxic green against the frosty turquoise accent lighting within. For a moment, I swore I glimpsed shoulders and a head wearing a thorny crown. I felt the fine hairs on my arms and neck stand tall, as though a gust of cold wind had just cut through me. There, where I thought I discerned a crowned head, two eyes met my gaze. They were unlike anything I had ever seen before: luminous pale blue sickles that almost conjured the likeness of Earth's mighty moon in a waning crescent.

Almost. But these lacked the majestic reassurance of a celestial fixture. Instead, they seethed with a frosty and foreboding malice.

The icy crescents regarded me carefully. They were cold, hateful candles, flickering faintly like a pair of eyes at the bottom of a deep well. So far away, yet somehow so close; at any moment they could reach out and drag me down into the roiling liquids of the starship's veins.

"Miss?"

"What," I cried out as I jumped to face the startled porter at my side.

"I'm sorry, didn't mean to give you a fright. I was just saying that there's been a problem with one of the baggage ships, so it might take a minute or two to get your luggage to you. But if you like, you can wait in the atrium while we sort it out."

"Oh, yes, that's quite all right," I stammered. "The atrium?"

"Yes, miss, just through those doors," he replied, pointing across the room.

"Thank you."

I glanced back at the bubbling tank. Nothing. Apart from its churning blue liquid, the tank was empty. Smoothing my blouse to compose myself, I turned around and strolled to the double doors my porter had pointed out. On either side of the intricate stained-glass panels stood two doormen. They nodded to me in unison and, with one sweeping motion, threw open the doors, bowing their heads as I entered.

What I now beheld was something for which I was completely unprepared. The instant I stepped through those doors I was blinded by a flood of intense golden light. Everything shimmered and gleamed in the cavernous hall.

Atrium, indeed. Ancient Catholic Cathedral would be the more accurate moniker. Windows on either side of the chamber stretched from the granite floors and soared up and up until they met, where they intertwined along the vaulted ceiling, creating a panorama of the stars. The overwhelming vista was interrupted at regular intervals by towering bulkheads of gilded bronze. The bulkheads were like ancient columns, with polished statues of gleaming bronze at their feet. Each statue was different: fantastic and bizarre likenesses of legends and myths from Terran antiquity. I recognized the nautical theme by the few figures I recognized: Homer, the poet of Ancient Greece, Neptune, the Roman God of the Sea, and Ferdinand Magellan, sixteenth-century explorer. The other five were not familiar to me. Silent and stoic they stood, holding aloft globes of resplendent light. In the face of all this, only one word was able to slip deftly past my lips.

"Impressive." I had to lean back so that I could take in the feat of metallurgy overhead. Twisted bronze arches were woven through the rafters like the fossils of some mammoth beast in a museum exhibition. Cords of copper and branches of bronze intersected with one another, disguising translucent pipes that pushed green and blue liquids back and forth. The lighting in the room shone through and around those busy pipes, bending in ribbons of color on everyone below. If I hadn't known better, I'd have thought we were on the bed of some enchanted lake.

The effect was hypnotizing, and I found myself following the current of bubbles from one tube to the next as they danced around in the rafters overhead. As my eyes followed those bubbles to a shadowy corner where the piping fed into a large tank, I caught a glimpse of glowing orbs again – amber yellow in hue this time – distorted by the water's current. Their light seemed to blink at me from that shadowy corner. I could not break my gaze with those piercing lights. Why weren't they moving with the current? The bubbles rushed by, but the orbs were steady. And light was not bending as though its source lay behind the pipes. I squinted trying to make up for the distance, trying to bring things into focus–

"This'll be your luggage, Miss," the porter said from behind me. He smiled, gesturing to a pimple-faced steward whose uniform looked two sizes too big. The young Terran smiled, adjusting the grip his spindly fingers had on my designer bags.

"Just follow me then; I'll carry your bags," the steward reassured.

"Very good," I said with a nod, trying to shake my mind fog. The porter bowed as we left, and the steward led me to the grand entryway, where the lifts shuttled crew and patrons alike to their onboard destinations.

When our turn came, we boarded a lift and I saw that it was comprised mostly of glass, which provided a view of the inner workings of the *Starship Ichthus*. After selecting 'Deck D' for me, the steward rode in silence. I stared off through the void of cables and piping, on the lookout for more shining orbs. Apparently, the lifts were not designed for speed, and the silence inside lingered for longer than was comfortable as we made our descent.

As the lift counted off each deck we passed, I examined its infoscreen. I had boarded on Deck B. One level above me, Deck A was labeled 'Command Bridge,' and its label glowed red atop the list of destinations. The lift counted off Deck B and Deck C... then Deck G lit up.

"Damnedest thing, ma'am," my steward said with the shake of his head. "Some genius put Deck G out of order. It's called Deck G because that's where all the Grand Luxury Suites are. Caused a lot of confusion during training, it did. But now, my brain's rewired to 'A, B, C, G.'" He turned to me with a particularly stupid grin. I feigned a laugh for him as Deck D lit up proudly in green. Only six passenger decks, I noticed. Interesting. There was a 'Deck F' button, but it had a digital security panel next to it. That suggested special access, which made sense. Lower decks were usually reserved for the ship's machine works. On big vessels with all their moving parts, full crews of mechanics were needed to service and maintain the engines.

"Now arriving on Deck D: First Class," the ship's automated hospitality voice informed us. The steward fumbled with my luggage as he hopped off the lift before me.

"What was the cabin number again, Miss?" asked the red-faced steward as he pulled my luggage into the elegant cream and scarlet corridor. I heard the distinct sound of sweaty skin peeling away from leather as the young man wrapped his clammy hands around my trunk for a better grip.

"Oh," I murmured as I opened my datapad and pulled up the itinerary. "D-1," I read off.

"By the bow, 'ey? Very posh."

He continued down the cream-white hall, his feet tramping along the thick, scarlet carpet. He reminded me of a fledgling penguin I'd once seen on assignment. The squat little bird had been scurrying after its parents in a blinding ice flow, fighting against the wind. My youthful steward had no such handicap.

"Just a little further this way," he reassured after a good five-minute walk. At length, we arrived outside my cabin.

"Go ahead and wave your datapad over the lock interface there," he said with a nod at the small console on my cabin door. I did as instructed and, with a dull thud and a high-pitched twitter, the door pushed back and slid silently into the wall. The dark maw of my cabin's entrance yawned wide, waiting for its first unwitting traveler.

"After you, Ms. Galikor," said the steward, spying my name on the security panel greeting message.

We stepped into the black void that I would call home for the next three weeks. The instant I crossed the threshold; the darkness was cast away by a wash of stunning light. I took a minute to absorb my surroundings.

Overall, I was pleased with my cabin. It was outfitted with all the desired accommodations: a bed, an entertainment console in the wall, and, of course, a port window, around which the sitting area was arranged.

The circular window was cut into the starboard side of the bow, offering a stunning view of the journey ahead. The space was much roomier than I was expecting and, all said, it was a very competent attempt at comfort.

Perhaps it is my own bias poking its nasty head above water, but I was disappointed to find that there was not a single lamp or table light, but only the overheads, which were programmed with a dimmer.

Cliptorgian[5] passengers need an alternative. It is stress-inducing to drown in a shower of light every time we return to our domicile. That has just as much to do with biology as it does with psychology. So often, Terran designers seem to need constant reminding that not all their passengers are human.

---

[5] Originally nocturnal, Cliptorgians are a humanoid mammal that evolved looking up at the night sky and advanced to the stars much sooner than humans. A societal matriarchy, Cliptorgians rarely resort to violence and find the masculine-centric ways of Earth fascinating. They were the first to colonize the Outer Rim worlds of Hierrnaus and Heiznaus but lost both within twenty years to the transgressions of invading Candalonians in that sector. Those same skirmishes started the War of Formation.

As Cliptorgians, our adaptability can lead us astray. We forget to care for our natural requirements. We are, after all, night-eyed beings by nature, though we've allowed ourselves to lose sight of that. Centuries of adaptation alongside Hulgarians[6] and Terrans have resulted in our solar-centric cycle. Today, we've all but abandoned our nocturnal patterns, save our biannual solstice holidays, for which our celebrations run from sun-down to sun-up.

Those lunar influences still permeate our living habits. Our private chambers, for example, are not riots of illumination. Instead, they are places of soft tranquility, bathed in deep purples punctuated by gentle swathes of richest emerald. Illumination emanates from slender strips of faint light which climb the curved walls and converge into patterns of twinkling lights overhead.

It was in such a room that I said goodbye to my wife, Seyva, only days before. For the first time, she asked me not to go. "They can send somebody else. I miss waking up beside you," she said. I missed that too. And I had missed so much: anniversaries, birthdays, nights lying awake talking…

I hadn't been happy with the travel aspect of my work for a long time. The further away I got, the more

---

[6] Hulgarians evolved in the swamplands of Cliptorgia as amphibious creatures with rich cultural ties to the oceans and billabongs of their home world. Hulgarians take great pride in fueling research in the ISF and are deeply invested in the equal treatment of all sentient life forms.

often Seyva's face invaded my thoughts. The desire to reach out and embrace her ached in my chest.

"Apologies again for the luggage delay," the steward said from behind me.

Well, I thought, I swam through that mental maelstrom of thoughts fairly quickly. "It was really no trouble to me," I recovered, turning to offer him a polite smile. "I hope it wasn't to you. As I understand it, one of the baggage ships had difficulties?" I was sure to phrase it as a question, and I was even more careful to ask as innocently as possible.

"Yes, yes, that's right. Still a few gremlins to flush out, I'm afraid," he chortled with a wink.

Gremlins. That didn't sound very pleasant. Or technical. In my experience, 'gremlins' was the non-technical, highly superstitious term sailors used for issues with a ship's functions. Such things were more closely related to inexplicable bad luck than to any technical diagnosis.

"If there won't be anything else, I'll take my leave," he added. I wasn't entirely sure if that was a question or a confident declaration of intent. I supposed I'd let the little fellow off the hook.

"I should be fine for the moment, thank you," I said, reaching for my datapad on the dresser. I queued up a tip for transfer – just a few digits[7] for his trouble – but as I turned back to ask for his courtesy number, I heard the door seal up in the wake of his exit.

---

[7] Official currency of the Interplanetary Space Federation.

Never in my fifteen years of travel have I ever known a steward, porter, or any other crew member to leave without lingering at least a few seconds in anticipation of a tip.

How very strange, indeed.

3. THE CAPTAIN

July 7th, A.D. 2299
00:05 IST

Thud, thud, thud.

I looked to the cabin door. Or more accurately, I leapt to my feet and fixed my gaze so intently on the cabin door that it felt as if I would blast it open with the slightest twitch of my eyes.

Although it had not even been thirty minutes, it was now well after midnight. I had opened my luggage to unpack, then landed in one of my two accent chairs. I had to talk myself out of using the minibar to unwind, choosing instead to sip mindlessly on a tonic water. There, I had zoned out, lost in thought as my gaze wandered aimlessly through my view of the stars. Memories of past trips drifted through my conscience, and I stayed planted there until the knock at my door shook my meandering thoughts loose with a start.

The room shook again with those same three rolling knocks.

"Coming," I said, trying not to sound too annoyed. For the sake of discretion, I flipped the lid back down on my suitcase. Unpacking would have to wait. As I tapped the key panel and the door slid open, my mouth began forming my reply; a firm and vibrant, "Yes?"

Unfortunately, my monosyllabic response collapsed into a faint gasp of air. There I stood, face to face with a giant amongst Terrans; quite possibly the tallest human male I had ever seen. His frame, lanky yet broad in the shoulders, stretched to either side of the doorway and his eyes, dark and piercing from under his officer's cap, stared down at me with a quiet but intent malevolence.

Or so it seemed to me, under the shadow of that stone-faced titan's rigid brow. He was well over two meters tall, his skin appeared dull and grey, like some stone gargoyle. He dipped his head under the top of the doorframe to get a closer look at me. His dark eyes gleamed under the brim of his cap as they probed my face for secrets.

"Miss Galikor?" His voice was a tall, sonorous drone, with an accent that made him sound like he was carrying a few rocks in his gullet.

"Ms. Galikor," I tried politely.

"First Officer Graves," he flourished his left hand, placing it open on his chest. His hand was massive when he spread it wide, like an albino bat launching out of his uniform. "I'm here to escort you to the captain. He says you have an interview?"

"Oh, yes. Indeed. I'm glad to hear that was cleared. Let me just–"

"Quickly now. The captain is a very busy man, and he is ready for you now. If you'll follow me."

I shook my head and grabbed my datapad, then bolted after my escort.

Officer Graves was already to the end of the corridor by the time I locked my cabin door and caught my breath. Sensing no footsteps behind him, he had finally glanced back and turned on his heel, standing there like a stringent schoolteacher waiting for a tardy pupil.

"This is only a courtesy, Miss Galikor. The captain has many things to oversee due to our departure delays."

"I realize that, and I'll be grateful for whatever time he can spare me."

"Thank you. I knew you'd understand. Your agency explained that you were very seasoned... very professional. The captain tries very hard to keep his appointments, but I'm sure you see how, in the face of the ship's delays, fraternizing with travel writers is not a matter of the utmost importance. Miss."

That last one was on purpose; I had no doubt.

Never mind my schoolteacher metaphor; a prison guard would be a more apt descriptor. I'd dealt with his type before. Never a thought to public relations. Judging by his age and rank, he had served with the company a good number of years. With such an affable personality, I suspected he had hit his professional ceiling and was unlikely to advance further. Certainly not to, say, the position of captain. Not only does one need a head for command and knowledge of spacefaring technologies, but also the temperament of a world-class maître d.

Onward and upward we went, climbing through a circuit of crew-only stairwells kept cheery with ivory paint and bronze metalwork accents. This went on for far too long. If Graves was in such a hurry, why not take the lifts?

Finally, we arrived at the topmost deck of that massive vessel in relative silence, with only Officer Graves' faint grumbles to break the monotony. The stairwell ended, spitting us out into the grand casino which took up the rear half of Deck A. From there, Graves led me to an armored door, where he waved his ID over the lock. I had only a few seconds to glance behind me at the plush gold and Devil's Food Cake velvet of the sparkling casino.

Perhaps I would come back to enjoy the space, I told myself.

Graves led me through the thick security door and onto the observation deck, which was a long, hallway with tall ceilings and bay windows that offered a view of the ship's port broadside. It was a vast room with a view so grand, it seemed designed to make me feel inferior.

On most ships, space was utilized efficiently, and

designs which blended seamlessly with the public rooms were favored. Such choices provided passengers with a sense that they were merely in a grand hotel in a modern city. But *Ichthus* had intense corners, mysterious gaping channels, and endless shadows. It was designed to remind passengers that it was a mechanical being, moving and churning and muscling everyone through space. It was obvious, yet still dark and secretive in some mysterious way.

Was it a trick of the mind because the vessel was so immense? Perhaps. At the very least, that's what I settled on to prevent more unease from trickling into the back of my mind.

At last, we stood outside the command bridge. It was a deckhouse overlooking the vessel's grandiose bow, fitted with all manner of control stations. There were consoles for astronomy and navigation, consoles for steerage with levers and a helm, and consoles for security and administration. Out and over either side of the ship, walkways led to globular lookout-posts for surveying the hull and length of the vessel; sailors called them bridge wings.

In front of the broad, square windows on the forward-facing bulkhead stood the captain himself, checking off something or other on an illuminated datapad. By even a cursory glance, he was nothing like the ghoulish Mr. Graves. Instead, the captain was shorter, though no less commanding, with a rotund belly tucked neatly under his carefully arranged officer's coat. His face was softened by his well-manicured white beard, and his brow was only lightly dusted with worry lines.

I noted that his mustache was streaked with fading red hair, which accented his wide smile. Officer Graves and I walked out onto the deck to greet him.

"Graves! I see you've brought me a friend," he boomed merrily, striding over to us and clapping a none-too-amused Mr. Graves on the shoulder with a jolly chuckle. "I hope he didn't scare you too much."

"No, no," I replied, "your *Fifth* Officer was most pleasant and helpful."

"Fifth Officer?" The captain scratched his head, his pleasant demeanor breaking slightly.

"Oh, no! Is it First Officer? I'm so sorry," I feigned with a side-eye to Graves. "I'm still a bit travel weary from back-to-back assignments." I played it off with an innocent chuckle.

Graves's face suggested that he was ready to crumple me up and stuff me directly into the nearest footlocker. He might have, too, had we been alone. Thankfully that was not the case.

"If that's all you need of me, sir, I've got to clear up this baggage mess now or I fear we'll be delayed even further." Graves was clenching his teeth so hard that I expected to hear one crack.

"Yes, of course, of course," the captain replied, his face returning to its jovial state. He waved Graves off. "As you were."

Graves nodded and, avoiding eye contact with me, took his leave. As he was departing, I noted that he met up with a handful of deck crew in the hallway. They handed him what looked like a shock-stick[8] before everyone tramped off together.

No, that couldn't be right. What in the world would a first officer need a shock-stick for? That is, apart from leaning into an irksome writer's prison guard metaphor. I admit that I only spotted it for a moment, but I could have sworn... And those crewmen, as they disappeared down a flight of stairs, their bulky bodies appeared to be heavily armored in some kind of riot gear.

"Tell me, Ms." the captain trailed off, "erm, Galidoor, is it?" He smiled meekly.

"Galikor," I said. "With a 'K' in the middle," I replied nonchalantly while creating a new audio recording on my own datapad.

The captain gestured for me to walk with him along the command bridge. "Galikor," he nodded. "Yes, yes. Terribly sorry!" Delicately, he offered his hand in formal greeting. "Captain Eugene Englehorn at your service!" His enthusiasm overtook gentility as he pumped my arm with his charismatic handshake. "So, what would you like to know about our floating slice of paradise?"

I smiled at his simple rhyme.

"Do you like that," he asked eagerly. "That's my own little concoction. You can use it, of course, but I'd

---

[8] A nightstick with an electrified, cattle-prod-like tip. This controversial weapon was considered a humane alternative to firearms for security battalions aboard public spaceships.

love for it to be a direct quote. I think a good captain should be as sharp in his wits as he is in his judgement."

"I'll take it under consideration," I said, laughing earnestly at his giddy charm. "But I was specifically curious about some of the inner workings of the *Ichthus*: the propulsion system, a total crew count, the different crew functions… any newly patented mechanics being utilized?"

"Wait now," the captain said, holding his hand up to stop me as a slim shadow fell over his face, "I thought you were a travel writer. Shouldn't you be more concerned with passenger accommodations, onboard amenities, and the like." It was a statement, not a question.

"Well, yes, that's the usual fare, and my article will certainly include all that but, for one reason or another, my readership includes a growing number of gearheads and technophiles. So, I don't mean to catch you off guard, but I do hope we can oblige them. Admittedly, I wasn't too keen on having to write about it at first, but I've actually found it invigorating to figure out what makes these vessels tick, so to speak." I smiled sweetly.

"Oh, well, that's refreshing. I always say people ought to take more interest in what we do to make these monsters *go*. The only thing is…"

He trailed off, twiddling his thumbs between clasped fingers as we stared out one of the globular lookout orbs.

"Yes," I leaned in to encourage his secret.

"I'm not really at liberty to discuss the nitty-gritty.

Not with *Ichthus*. Her funding was a private venture, and as such, there are far too many company secrets… gumming up the works. Proprietary secrets, I'm sorry to say."

That was odd. Most cruise companies couldn't wait to divulge the details of their newest wonder-ship. The captain seemed an affable-enough older gentleman, perhaps a bit of charm would aid my cause.

"You can't tell me even a little bit? Just enough to whet my readers' appetites," I coaxed, as I laid my right hand gently on his right arm.

The captain chortled as he, just as gently, placed my hand back on my datapad.

Grimtash[9].

"No, no, I'm afraid not. Non-disclosure agreements and all. Far above my pay grade, anyway." He waved at some invisible mosquito. "I'm sure you understand?"

"Of course," I replied. I smiled, trying to match his casual attitude while subconsciously brushing a strand of hair back over my ear.

It was worth a try, at any rate.

"No worries at all, Ms. Galikor," he reassured.

"Why don't you tell me everything you can, and I won't press beyond that," I suggested.

---

[9] A Cliptorgian curse originating from root words 'grim' (star) and 'tash' (dust/soot/mess), this ancient planetary slur is used as versatilely as the English word 'fuck.' It is thought to have originally expressed 'nonsense,' such as the Terran terms 'balderdash' or 'hogwash.'

He snickered a little. "I can tell you my favorite feature of this mechanical monstrosity is her autopilot capabilities. That's technical, I suppose. Er, watch this!"

Captain Englehorn pressed a button on the console that sat front and center in the middle of his command bridge. The whole workstation stood alone and housed a massive wooden steering wheel. If it was not an antique, it was an astounding imitation.

"Is this real wood," I asked with a little gasp of admiration.

"Aye," the captain said, wiggling his mustache proudly at me. "Beautiful, isn't she?"

"Indeed," I said with a nod.

"And…" he reached for a small number-pad on the workstation, where a block of nine square yellow buttons glowed. He pressed the button dead center in the middle of the pad, and the entire console before us raised a meter, lifted by hydraulics in the floor.

There, in the center of the floor, in a glowing green compartment, was the most beautiful square of copper pipework I had ever seen.

"Activate *Starship Ichthus* Autopilot. Voice ID pattern: Captain Englehorn."

The captain waited a moment, and the console beeped with approval. Then, the copper pipes shifted, zapped to life by the ship's computer. It was a simple android, which unfolded and stepped out before us. When it was done reshaping into a humanoid, it stood a meter-and-a-half tall. It was alarmingly skeletal, and it had no face, save two glowing eyes, which cast the same rich amber light as its num-pad controls.

"Ms. Galikor, *this* is Auto. Not just a worthy bridge companion, but a fully autonomous autopilot!" Then, leaning close to my ear, he added, "Best damn co-pilot I ever had, too."

I laughed as the robot saluted me and the console lowered back into the floor with a creak behind us.

"How marvelous," I exclaimed.

"Auto," the captain beamed, "please take command of the bridge while I escort Ms. Galikor to the lifts."

"Aye, Captain," Auto bowed slightly, saluting us both, then an alert echoed over the loudspeaker. "Attention," Auto's amplified voice soothed, "this is Autopilot. Please be aware the captain has relinquished command to me. As a result, all manual controls in steerage and navigation shall be inoperable until I am relieved of duty. If your department has been affected by my control, you are entitled to a short break. You will be asked to return to your post when necessary. If your department is not affected, please carry on with your work."

"I could take a whole day off," the captain bragged quietly to me. "And no one would grumble, because half the bridge crew gets the day off with me. As a team leader, I think Auto is absolutely brilliant!"

"It's hard to disagree with you, even just with this short demonstration," I said.

We stood there, our chuckles dying down, before

I finally felt the awkwardness set in and decided I wouldn't have it.

"Thank you for your time. I so appreciate it, particularly with these gremlins you're still flushing out."

All the color drained instantly from the captain's face and his entire body went rigid: whether from fear or rage, I couldn't tell. Maybe both. His jaw tensed up and I barely noticed his shoulders hunch forward as his back muscles tightened with stress. His change from a jolly, lighthearted man to this quaking, white-faced husk was lightning-quick... and terrifying. Suddenly, Mr. Graves seemed no more threatening than a sour old Fallamon[10].

I don't know how long we stood there staring at each other, nor what exactly his reaction was supposed to mean. Finally, the captain's jaw relaxed ever so slightly, and his mouth cracked open. "Wherever did you get the impression our fine ship has *gremlins*?"

"My steward mentioned gremlins in the works... very playfully, I might add."

I nearly jumped straight out of my shoes as the captain gave a planet-shattering belly–laugh. He patted me vigorously on the shoulder until his cheeks

---

[10] Very little is known about Fallamon due to their distrust of other species. Indigenous to the Fallorien Forest on the Outer Rim world of Hierrnaus, these bipedal, shell-backed reptiles have a one-meter stature and an average lifespan of 220 years. Fallamon are fiercely materialistic and relish in re-appropriating ISF goods. Their broods are often found living in barns, scrap yards, and even landfills within the colonized sectors of their home world.

recovered their original rosy hue.

"Never heard the term."

"No," I asked. "I have. It's an old Terran term originating in the early twentieth century which suggests an undetermined technical malfunction. I'm summarizing, of course, but that's the gist of it."

"That's the gist of it, huh," the captain asked with sudden severity. "I assure you, Ms. Galikor, I've never heard our sailors use that term. All due respect; it's a late night for everyone. I think you need some rest." Something in him had shifted. He turned to a young Cliptorgian woman at a corner console. "Quartermaster Rohkla, would you kindly escort Ms. Galikor to the passenger lifts on this deck? I suddenly find myself needed elsewhere."

"At once, sir," Rohkla replied, nodding at me and extending her arm to the doorway behind us.

"Thank you again," I echoed weakly to the captain.

As Quartermaster Rohkla led me down the hallway, my ears pricked, catching a few growling words from the captain before the command bridge sealed behind us. I distinctly heard him say, "You find that goddamned drunk and get him up here *now!*"

And so, there was our true Captain. His façade of professionalism was washed away by a flash flood of emotions. He was no different than the sea tyrants of Terran history who meted out a cruel life on ocean waves. Further proof that there was, without a doubt, something fishy about the *Ichthus*. It was no ordinary ship.

Why had the word 'gremlins' made the captain malfunction like an outdated robot? And why the secrecy regarding the ship's tech specs?

In that moment, the ember of curiosity burning deep within my brain flickered into a burgeoning flame. How could I have guessed then at the firestorm of answers headed my way?

4. DINING

Upon returning to my cabin, I sat with my datapad, recording written notes for a bit while I waited for the computer to process the transcription of my interview with Captain, adding details so I wouldn't forget. After some time at the desk, however, my eyes drooped, pining for sleep. I turned in for the night.

When I awoke, the time on my console startled me; it was well after lunchtime. In fact, it was three minutes past the fourteenth hour. Dear me, I thought. The apparentness of 'time as a concept' was ever imposing on a long cruise through space, but even still, I had slept for ten full hours!

I sat up in bed and grabbed my datapad, opening my notes from before. It was my habit to read through things as soon as I got up from a long slumber, for it helped me with revisionary thoughts. However, that ritual only lasted five minutes before my stomach let out a groan.

The noise cued in me an inkling of hunger, and I knew it would only be a matter of minutes before that hunger crippled my mood *and* my physical being. I was not a being who could go hungry. I simply didn't function.

My formal dinner had been a sandwich at the Embarkation Station the night before, so I decided to explore the nearest dining amenities.

I took a moment to powder my nose and cheeks, using larkha[11] to accentuate the silver hue that marked healthy Cliptorgian freckles. My sense was that the patrons around me aboard *Starship Ichthus* had a formal air. I dared not go out without looking my best.

I got ready for a good ten minutes, just enough so that I felt confident in my efforts. Then, I set up my room's retina-lock and tested it twice for assurance that I could get back in before setting off to find a food court. The itinerary included a map of all decks, and I was disappointed to find that there were no dining options on Deck D. I dared not try my luck on the upper decks, not while the ship was still boarding. Thankfully, there was a small food court one deck below me. No doubt it had been included to mitigate complaints such as the ones brewing in my head.

---

[11]A powder makeup made of ground silver shells, which can be found along the midland shores of Cliptorgia. The custom of male and female Cliptorgians powdering their cheeks with larkha dates back to early modern times in Cliptorgian society, some nine hundred years ago as of the writing of this piece [A.D. 2319].

Remembering my way to the lifts, I called for one in descent, and rode just one level down to Deck E. The lift arrived with a ding, and I ducked inside. I looked out at the tangle of mechanics that the clear glass cylinder offered me. Green and blue lights pulsated across the winding maze of moving parts: piping, wiring, gears, and pistons all working in concert with one another. Steam huffed from exhaust ports, the pure white smoke gathering like cumulus clouds urged forward by the breath of giants.

It was then that I realized the primary design statement on the *Starship Ichthus*: water. It was caught there in various physical forms, namely as liquid and as steam, thrumming through the pipes all around. It was a reminder of our common bond as sentient creatures – water made up most of our physical forms. That lifeforce molecule somehow comprised us all, despite the great distance between our worlds.

Another ding. "Please allow passengers to exit the lift first," said the friendly, disembodied voice. I was instantly thankful for it as I stepped off the lift and into a crowd of eager Terran passengers clutching hot dogs. They still had their luggage. As I rounded the corner to the dining kiosks on Deck E, I realized a good number of passengers still carried their luggage.

Strange, I thought. That's why I'm an advocate of boarding drills with a new ship's concierge crew. *Ichthus* made the news in my own circles when *To the Stars* announced they'd be moving up the new ship's maiden voyage. It seemed now that cutting back on concierge training was causing problems.

At least my food would be ready fast, I told myself. I was less likely to have to wait very long for anything because the cooks would be on edge from the strangely timed dining rush. I smiled with satisfaction; my luggage and room were already settled and cared for. It was an encouraging start.

Despite the gothic facades of each storefront, I recognized the names as typical food chains, including Feh'tok, the place to go off-world for traditional Cliptorgian grub. They played the Terran business game best, or so I'd been told more than once. I wandered over and ordered pan-shee, a favorite dish from home. It was a soup-base with noodles and root vegetables, plus a zing of spice to clear the sinuses. With all the moisture hanging in the air aboard the *Starship Ichthus*, it felt like a damp and rainy day. My body craved the soup.

As I had hoped, it was ready in minutes… and it was fresh. I sat and enjoyed my pan-shee, which was admittedly more watered down than was my preference. I always forgot they made it from a southern recipe. This also meant there were a few fresh meatballs of the pungent gorb.

Gorb were a fat, tiny sour fish native to the swamps and mudbanks of equatorial Cliptorgia and found in nearly all dishes, Hulgarian and Cliptorgian alike. Gorb was once the mark of a Hulgarian dish, but our two cultures first blended in those warm bogs so long ago that it's unclear who first used gorb for nourishment. As a northerner, I found the sour gorb and the extra watery broth unpleasant. I liked my noodles to soak up more water and hold more of the brothy flavor. I wanted only a small, salty puddle to lap up at the end of my meal, rather than a long drink with flakes of chum.

Still, the moisture in the air pressed in, chilling my bones, so I plucked the gorb out of my broth and tried masking the sour fish flavor by dumping a packet of extra spices into my bowl. It worked, even singeing my nostrils, and prompting my nose to drip. I could drink only a sip, though, then dabbed my nose off before deciding to get in line for a warm beverage. It was better than having a full dessert of some sort, even if I did get one of those awful sugary Earth things – which I was not going to do.

"Ladies and gentlemen," the loudspeakers announced proudly, "this is Captain Englehorn speaking. We'd like to invite you to celebrate our departure with one of my favorite traditions."

Zirkrum[12], I thought. I slept all that time, and we still hadn't departed? I shook my head as I listened to the captain continue over the loudspeakers.

"Each captain here at *Red Dwarf Starliners* has their

[12] Thought to originate from the root words 'zir' (bird) and 'krum' (feces), this Cliptorgian cuss has no apparent genesis. The most popular theory points to the species' prehistory, when large predatory falcons preyed on the Cliptorgian species during daylight hours. Etymology suggests that the term originated as declaration of a nearby predator and fell into use as a colorful exclamation over time.

own song to launch a maiden voyage. No matter the ship, it's up to her captain to play her out of port. So, let's get this party started!"

The loudspeakers wailed the introductory chords to some centuries-antiquated classical rock group from Earth. People around me cheered, tapping feet or bobbing heads. One human woman murmured the lyrics along with the song, though it was clear she did not know many of them. I tried to tune the crowd noise out.

At last, the *Starship Ichthus* fired her engines and backed us out of the locks at Embarkation Station.

I waited in line at a stand near the grand hallway, which offered exits to the passenger section of Deck E, and a view of Cliptorgia as it receded from view behind us.

The food kiosk I awaited was advertising fresh krā, a frothy orange Hulgarian tea. Unlike the line for my meal, though, this vendor seemed to have slowed into the post-rush lull, for I was three people deep in line for a good long while. Patiently, I rocked back and forth to keep my joints fresh, at which point I leaned back and noted the clear pipes with ornate brass fittings running along the ceiling and down the walls, pumping dark blue-green liquid through them… and there, in the dark corner nearest me, was a pair of icy blue eyes.

The massive clear pipe, easily as wide in diameter as my own shoulders, was no more than two meters from my little dining table there in the food court.

Despite the rushing, discolored water foaming inside, I had no doubt what I was seeing. Much closer now, they were surely pupils, because I instantly had the impression of a head. Next, I saw the light of the eyes dip out as their owner blinked.

"You," I felt myself mutter, though I admittedly did not hear my words take form beyond a grumble. The eyes shifted, then ducked around an elbow joint in the pipes. Without a second thought, I hopped out of line and bolted after them.

5. TURNED AROUND

The shadow in the pipes: I recall chasing it through two red hallways, each separated by wooden doors, each plush with burgundy Brocatelle Jacquard carpet on the walls and beautiful cedarwood flooring. The classical rock song thrummed over the loudspeakers as I gave chase, which only drove me forward faster.

The shadow zipped through the pipe up along the ceiling, then swung left around a blind bend. I just kept following the pipes. My sense of direction told me I was heading to stern, but beyond that, the ship's pipes guided me. Like the veins of *Ichthus*, I had no doubt those coolant pipes were leading me to the vessel's heart: the engines.

It was then that I turned the corner and met a most peculiar person, but one I had a good feeling about. He was an older man, his body tough and knotted like hard wood. His goatee of grey hair and bulbous, pock-marked nose told me he was human, but if that hadn't given him away, I may have mistaken his milky white complexion for Cliptorgian.

I had encountered many pale interstellar travelers who, when denied the yellow light of Sol, did indeed look like members of my own species. He was slumped in a folding chair, snoring gently with arms crossed over his chest. The brim of his khaki fishing hat drooped over his eyes; perhaps he was hiding here for an on-duty nap, I suspected, noting his coveralls. They were the same deep green as those worn by the porters I had encountered, though this old sailor lacked the coattails. He was most likely a technician.

As I took a few steps closer, he stirred.

"Whazzat," he murmured as his heavy breathing caught in his throat.

"Oh, so sorry," I said, feigning innocence. "I must've gotten myself turned around."

"So long as ye' don't mention ya' caught me sleeping on the job, I won't cause a fuss. Yer' pretty lost if yer' down here, though."

"I'm afraid I am," I said, maintaining my story. "I was... following something."

"Oh," the old-timer said, lifting the brim of his hat with his hand. His bushy eyebrows wriggled like caterpillars. "What do you mean by that?"

Just then, I noticed a circular hatch in the floor under his chair. Perhaps that's what he was guarding, I thought. There was nothing menacing in his tone, but once again I had the sense that something aboard the

Ichthus was stowed away in secrecy. I took a chance.

Leaning in, I decided to divulge half the truth. He perked up as I closed the proximity between us.

"I saw something glowing in the tubes," I said. No sense telling him I thought they'd been eyes. I shivered, recalling how they'd leered at me.

"Interesting," he said. The old human scratched his chin, his fingers prodding through his sparse and wiry hairs there. "And it was headed this way?"

"That's right," I nodded. I noticed that the pipe I'd been following stopped traveling the length of the ceiling, turned at a ninety-degree elbow joint, then ran straight down into the floor behind the old-timer's chair. "It was moving through this tubing," I added, pointing at the pipes.

He wrinkled up his face. "That doesn't sound right."

"I know what I saw," I asserted.

"Oh, yes, yes," he nodded emphatically. "I don't mean I doubt you, but if you saw something glowing in the coolant, I may have my work cut out for me." I noted his hand move instinctually to the hilt of his sword. Strange, I thought. A maintenance man armed with a sword on his toolbelt.

Was it a toolbelt?

I noted a wrench, measuring tape, and a pouch for holding hardware… the sword seemed out of place.

"Well," he finally said, shaking himself from whatever equation rattled around in his brain, "I best get you back to the ship's more civilized sectors."

Questions raced through my mind, but I resolved to acquiesce in hopes it might gain me an ally. "Of course," I said with a subtle bow in his direction. As he guided me back the way I'd come, I made note of every turn, observing that we were leaving 'Aft Deck E.' I had unwittingly chased those eyes all the way to the mechanical sectors at stern.

We chatted all the way, and I soon learned my chaperone was armed with more than just a sword; he possessed an arsenal of stories from a lifetime of interstellar travel. Artemis Bounty was his name, but his friends called him 'Pappy.' It was some joke nickname bestowed on him while he was serving in the Interstellar Navy. He'd enlisted to join during the Outer Rim Rebellion back in 2238, which made him nearly eighty years old, by my quick estimation. From there, he managed to transition to mechanical work aboard commercial vessels: his way to see the universe without staying in the armed forces, "which was a buttoned-up, tight-assed operation, ma'am, if you don't mind my saying."

I laughed. By then, he'd escorted me to the midship lifts.

"Thank you again," I said to Pappy as the doors opened. I stepped inside.

"Any time," he said. "I'll keep an eye out for those glowing orbs."

I stuck my arm out to hold the lift doors open. "You believe me," I asked, admittedly surprised at myself. Reflex had compelled me.

"I know an honest person when I meet one," he said with a smirk. "I'd say 'Don't be a stranger,' but passengers shouldn't be wandering around the aft decks."

"Well, perhaps I'll see you around," I tried. After all, he was an interesting fellow, and clearly an experienced sailor. No doubt he could provide me with some intriguing stories of past travels, and I was privately in the process of collecting such stories for a book I was slowly piecing together.

He just chuckled. "No," I pressed, "seriously. Let me buy you lunch tomorrow. I'd love to record some of your stories. I write about starships."

The lift dinged in agitation as I held the door. "Stand clear of the closing doors, please," an automated voice commanded me.

"Tomorrow at noon," I urged.

"Ah," he caved, "all right. Tomorrow at noon in the aft dining hall. Deck B. They've got the best-stocked bar."

"Perfect," I said. I withdrew my arm, and the lift doors snapped shut. Aft dining hall on Deck B, I repeated in my head so as not to forget.

'Noon,' according to Terrans, was midday on Earth, when Sol was at its zenith over the local meridian in the planet's sky. Because Cliptorgia was slightly larger than Earth, but rotated only a fraction faster than it, our days worked out to be only ninety-five minutes and thirty-two seconds longer. When Cliptorgians and Terrans had forged their alliance, my people chose to adapt several components of Terran culture, including measurements of time. We were more amenable, more open to adapting alongside creatures unlike ourselves. It was a benefit of the balance struck with Hulgarians on our mutual homeworld long ago. Considering the stubbornness of humans that plagued every form of society in our modern times, I often wondered if that was for the best. Terrans had no sibling consciousness, at least not on a level most of them could perceive. And they'd developed a bad habit of rugged individualism during their struggles with each other.

When I found my cabin, I marked the twelfth hour in my schedule assistant. I changed into my bahdok – a soft tunic of vegetable fiber from the bahrō plant of my hometown. On a previous assignment, a fellow passenger who specialized in Terran fabrics compared it to a much softer jute.

I could tell I was homesick by the number of notes wherein my thoughts wandered to my cultural heredity. The more I pondered Cliptorgian history and traditions, the more it meant I was suppressing my emotional desire to be home.

With a heavy sigh, I rolled onto my other side, hoping it would roll me away from such thoughts. My mind continued to wander down strange corridors until I dozed off.

6. ARTEMIS 'PAPPY' BOUNTY

July 8th, A.D. 2299
08:58 IST

As I slept that first night of the voyage, those orbs came back to haunt me in my sleep. They appeared above my bed, looking down from glass piping. Somewhere deeper, I knew that detail of my room to be false: a fabrication in my dream world. In the waking world, that was solid duct work, for the vent pushed cool, filtered air down on me. It was that detail that served to pull me back to the waking world, but not before the orbs morphed into two predatory eyeballs, bloodshot with cobalt pupils. The water around them glowed a sickly toxic green, and a clawed flipper lashed out for me from the shadows.

I awoke in a fog, and I did not feel rested. For that reason, I was left with the impression that I had several more hours to try and sleep. However, my bedside console struck nine in the morning, and reluctantly I shook the grog of sleep away.

Instantly, I sought to put thoughts to words. I took breakfast alone in my quarters as I recorded my first impressions of the vessel. I wanted to do so while it was fresh in my mind. Breaking only to refill my water, I accomplished my writing task by ten-thirty, then found myself anxious for lunch with the mysterious Pappy.

Ship crewmen tended to be cagey around journalists. And Pappy was an experienced sailor, so he'd probably be harder to fool. I needed a lie; nothing too complex… just something adjacent to the truth to make him comfortable. If I told him I was writing a review of the onboard experience, it would set off alarm bells.

My mind reached back into memories. When I first started my career, I worked at a periodical that had a young Terran woman writing the fluff culture pieces. It was all Grimtash, and she knew it, but she preferred calling it 'Lifestyle Advice.' Perhaps it was best to keep it that simple.

Since I'd been confined to my rooms all morning, I decided to put extra effort into cleaning up for the day. I didn't know how long I'd stay out on the social decks after lunch. In my experience, it was best to be ready for a full day out.

I chuckled at myself. Cabin fever must already be setting in… or was that just my curiosity?

At last, it was twenty minutes to noon, and I

headed to my rendezvous. As I reached the lifts, I joined a group of passengers waiting their turn for a ride. I was clearly caught up in the foot traffic of the luncheon hour. Creatures of all the known creeds, planets, and classes mingled shoulder to shoulder through the busy corridor, patiently waiting their turn for a free lift. Truly, there was even a clutch of three very well-dressed Fallamon sporting coattails and top hats. One of them even wore a monocle! I'd never seen such a spectacle.

Seeing as I had an appointment to keep, I pushed ahead determinedly without being rude. Politely, I excused myself when I had to. Whereas there was no trouble in navigating the ship, the social decks were so crowded with passengers milling about that it impeded my progress significantly, and I arrived nearly ten minutes late.

Pappy was already there, stooped over a glass of whiskey at the bar. His glass was half empty, and he seemed deep in thought. I didn't recognize him until I approached, for his profile was shrouded by a floppy bucket hat. His crow's feet scrunched, exaggerated by his rosy cheeks. Those esteemed wrinkles also, I noted, glistened where they had collected tears.

Registering his pensive demeanor, I approached cautiously so as not to give him a start. I sidled up next to him, lightly tapping his left arm to announce my arrival.

"I'm terribly sorry I wasn't here on time," I started. "I didn't think there would be such a crowd...

I suppose that's my fault for not realizing how busy the ship would be at lunchtime."

"Fine by me, so long as you don't mind that I got started without you." Pappy grinned, taking a generous swig of his drink. I noted the lonely ball of ice in his glass as he lowered it to the bar. He was already a drink in, and judging by his breath, whiskey was 'his poison,' as old Terrans liked to say.

Hard liquor at midday certainly went down like poison for me. But to see Pappy's flagrant disregard for drinking etiquette flooded me with selfish relief. The more he drank, the more likely he was to divulge the details of his current station.

And the more I got out of him, the more focused I'd be on the story. The more focused I was, the less inclined I'd be to have a drink myself. I was trying to avoid alcohol, working slowly towards sobriety before my intended career shift.

It was a prerequisite in my line of work to court people socially, and in an economy driven by Terran culture, sharing strong drinks was of paramount importance. As I had scaled back, I'd still found it necessary to start with a drink, thus putting my source at ease to do the same, too. But if Pappy hadn't needed that permission, then I certainly wasn't about to imbibe.

Pappy sniffled, rubbing at his nose with his hand.

"Are you okay," I asked him gently. "It looks like you've been crying."

"Just another tough shift," he said, waving it away.

"The whiskey loosens pressure on the waterworks," he half-chuckled, waving for the bartender.

"Oh, I'm sorry to hear it," I said, not sure what to make of that.

"Are you still feeling up to chatting?"

"Of course! I'm here, aren't I?"

"True enough," I said. I made a mental note not to make my pity known. Clearly, he was of the ilk who liked to 'tough it out' with problems, as the Terrans say. Not healthy, in my opinion, but then, neither was drinking hard liquor at noon.

"Anything that gets me away from that damned chair is a welcome distraction, to tell ye' the truth. Plus," he added, leaning in, "I need to talk to someone." He hesitated, ending his thought as he watched the barkeep saunter over. "Even if I *know* there's no right answer," he muttered quietly to himself.

"A refill for you, Pap?" The barkeep was chipper, his youthful eagerness plucking the tenor of his voice.

"Yes, sir. Please and thank you," Pappy said, sliding his glass closer. I watched as the young server popped the top off a fresh top-shelf whiskey. As the amber liquid cracked the ball of ice in Pappy's glass, I wondered if the 'keep was even old enough to drink alcohol.

Pappy held his glass up to the light dramatically. "Oh, God," he recited, "That men should put an enemy in their mouths to steal away their brains. That we should, with joy, pleasance, revel, and applause, transform ourselves into beasts!" He flashed me a wicked grin, gulped at his freshly refilled drink, and slammed the glass down triumphantly.

I raised an eyebrow and pointed. "Shakespeare?"

"Aye," Pappy beamed. "*Othello*, I think."

"Can I get you something, ma'am," the plucky barkeep asked. I ordered a flavored seltzer.

Pappy scoffed.

"It's a bit early for me personally," I explained with a smile.

The 'keep obliged my drink order, then wandered back down the bar. All the while, Pappy just stared into his drink. Finally, he sighed and said, "I don't know where to start."

"Take your time," I said. "Would it help if I asked a few questions?" He shook his head, took another swig of whiskey, then clunked his glass down to punctuate the gesture.

"Let's start with this monstrosity," he said, opening his arms to the room around us.

"The Aft Dining Hall," I asked, admittedly not following him.

"No!" he blurted out, then checked his volume. "The *Ichthus*," he clarified. I laughed at my own mistake, and it afforded Pappy a smile, too. "Let's see; do you know anything about interstellar reaction cores?"

"I know they power the ship's systems via contained nuclear reactions. And I know they get extraordinarily hot – particularly on larger vessels, where a larger core is needed to house multiple reaction chambers." I was eager to flex my knowledge, and I had Pappy grinning from ear to ear. He made a show of pointing his finger at me with excited approval, so I went on. "Now, housing a reaction core isn't that big a feat, but housing the proper cooling system is. On average, a reaction core's coolant system takes up about four times as much space as the rest of the engine. And designing the actual ship around that can be quite a challenge, which is why commercial freighters are so clunky and boxy."

"Shoot," Pappy crooned. "That's very good! I don't think I've ever met such a savvy dirtwalker[13]."

"Careful," I said playfully, "this dirtwalker spends more time in the stars than you might think."

He laughed, slapping his knee. "Well, then you'll understand why *Ichthus* is supposed to be so revolutionary. This ship has a state-of-the-art new cooling system: a HydroFuss. Hell, she's the only ship in the 'verse with it... for now, anyway. There's bound to be more, just as soon as they figure out how."

That made very little sense to me. If they'd designed this HydroFuss and it was working in the depths of *Ichthus*, what else was there to figure out? I couldn't tell if it was the liquor, or if Pappy's thoughts were growing cryptic.

"Slow down, you're moving too fast for me to

---

[13] Slang for a being who prefers to be 'grounded' on a planet or is not experienced at traveling through space for long distances. Comparable to the old Terran nautical slur 'landlubber.'

keep up," I told him. I was sure to say it playfully so as not to make him self-conscious about his drunken state. "What do they need to figure out about this HydroFuss system?"

He blinked very intentionally, which gathered the focus of both his eyes as they locked with my own.

"They need more slaves," he blurted out.

My mind raced. Was he a disgruntled employee? Surely, he didn't mean the ship literally relied on slavery of some kind. Such a notion in our modern times was downright draconian. Most of the personnel I'd seen onboard seemed moderately content. Were the mechanics working in poor conditions belowdecks, perhaps?

Pappy lifted his whiskey glass and snickered at himself. "Slaves... slaves of the clock. Slaves of the timecard. That's how this line of work can make you feel, but then..." His mutterings stalled out about there.

"I'm sorry, but I'm really not following you."

Pappy waved away some unseen flying pest. "Nah, you're fine. It's me. Shoulda' waited 'til you got here to star' drinkin'."

His words were slurring now. Perhaps he had had two drinks before my arrival? I decided to keep that question to myself. Instead, I shrugged. "No real harm done," I said, hiding my frustration. "Are you truly feeling up to this? You seem stressed."

"Well, with the new cooling system, there's been some, uh... unexpected troubleshooting," he explained, shifting as he paused. "Had a false alarm with it during boarding, even. That's what held up luggage distro!"

Interesting, I noted internally, recalling the delay with my own luggage. Though I admittedly was curious as to how the engines and the luggage were inexplicably connected.

"That was the *last* thing the deck officers wanted." Pappy cackled, remembering some scene he didn't share. Then, he tried for another swig of his drink, kicking his head back to drain the melted ice and traces of whiskey. He wrinkled his nose in disappointment, spying the empty glass, then waved down the barkeep again. Four fingers-worth of whiskey sloshed lazily into a fresh glass. The barkeep traded him the full glass in exchange for his empty one.

I caved in – ordered a cherry brandy. Cherry flavor was perhaps one of my personal favorite things from Earth. I had, when I was younger, spent a whole trip marveling over the various natural and unnatural variants of the flavor and fruit.

I would only have one, I told myself, and I would pace myself much better than Pappy. The strange old Terran had an alarmingly stout liver, even for an old sailor.

As the cherry brandy was set in front of me, Pappy signaled to the bartender.

"Hey, put that on mine, will ya'?"

"Oh, that's so kind, but not necessary," I interjected.

"No one was asking you," Pappy said playfully, swatting my datapad away from the bar tender.

"Well, okay then," I complied. "But back up a bit, because I'm not clear on something."

Jokingly, Pappy scooted his chair back from the bar a bit and smirked. "Sure," he said, waiting for my reaction.

I laughed with a shake of my head. "You said the luggage issue was caused by a problem with the engine coolant system. How so?"

"Ah," Pappy said just before tipping his glass again. His swigs were smaller now, savoring what was at least his third glass of whiskey. He nodded. "Rear luggage compartments had to be sealed off and redesigned as extra coolant tanks," Pappy explained.

"That doesn't quite add up," I pressed. "You see, along with several other passengers, I watched one of the luggage shuttles leave the belly of *Ichthus*.

Pappy's eyes grew wide.

"That same shuttle seemed to spiral out of control only to be shot down by a short-range fighter. Judging by the orange wingtip markings, I figured it was Orbital Guard."

The old Terran sailor's face went grim and white. His cheeks, however, refused to lose their rosy blossoms. "Working on a ship, even a big ship like this… it plays with you." He poked at the side of his head as he said it, indicating his brain. "Young sailors come aboard, they spend three months training and prepping for their first commercial cruise. They talk a big game because they're young. They want to get out and see the stars. But the two weeks before a voyage, that's crunch time. And crunch time can play tricks on your mind, especially if you've been sitting out in space, workin' yer' ass off while your own planet is winking back to you through every starboard porthole. You catch my meaning?"

"I imagine it can be taxing on the psyche, absolutely," I offered empathically. I could tell Pappy took a stubborn pride in his own mental fortitude. I was careful not to judge that in him. It was a survival tactic in his line of work.

"I seen it happen nearly every voyage. One or two technicians who spend too much time below decks get it in their head that they made the wrong decision. Convince a handful of mates to defect."

"Oh, my," I exclaimed. "You don't mean there were crewmembers shot down in that luggage shuttle."

He nodded somberly. "I most certainly do."

"Why were they killed?"

"They had taken armaments from a security post to force their way onto the luggage shuttle. They were deemed a threat to the whole station. At that point, our security detail backs off and Orbital Guard handles it."

I had no words. All I could do was shake my head. In all my years, I'd never heard of such a thing happening.

Pappy just stared up at the top shelf liquors behind the bar. He considered some new thought quietly, then sighed. "You have any kids," he asked point-blank.

I blinked. Seyva and I had certainly discussed it, but it was doubtful at our age. Cliptorgians did not require a male partner to reproduce biologically. However, chances of making the hormonal shift a female's body had to undergo in order to generate sperm in a single-sex partnership decreased significantly throughout our thirties. Once a female couple was past the age of forty, as Seyva and I were, it became increasingly more difficult. We hadn't even met until our early thirties, and we certainly weren't thinking about children for our first six years together. By the time we were finally married, I was already forty, and Seyva close behind me. I shared none of this, simply replied, "No."

"Not even a niece or nephew," Pappy clarified. Again, I shook my head. He nodded slowly. "I did. Had a little girl of my own. But staying in one place has never been an option for me. Wasn't then… isn't now. So, I took work and left, and I'd go back… ach." He waved the thought away as though it were a bad smell. "Eventually, they got tired of waiting for me to come home. Didn't tell me, mind you. Just up and left. The next time I showed up, they were gone."

I suspected that the excess rambling was due to emotions induced by his alcohol. He wasn't getting soggy and sad yet, though, so I said nothing.

With his next breath, Pappy stifled tears and sipped pitifully from his glass. "Sorry," he said, wiping his eyes.

"It's all right," I lied. I hated sad drunks.

"You remind me of her, that's all… or, what I hope she's like."

"Your daughter?" I was trying to stay supportive. If I pressed while he was emotional, it could backfire.

"Yeah. That's right. Sorry – I'm not makin' any sense."

I shook my head. "No sorry needed, friend."

He nodded, staring into his glass for a moment.

"Why'd you bring up children," I prodded, unable to make any connection.

"Huh? I thought you asked me?"

"No, sir," I said. "You brought up kids."

"Heh," he muttered as his lips shuffled for his next thought. "Been thinking about mine a lot lately on account of… well, on account of my protégé." He nearly whispered the word 'protégé,' divulging to me some undetected secret. Then, he leaned back in his seat with a subtle, stupid grin on his face.

I nodded, trying not to injure his pride.

"There's just nothing like that feeling: the feeling that a younger person looks up to ye' or considers your experiences to help them navigate life. And," he added demonstrably, "I don't even think it matters if they're the same species."

My chest tightened a bit. Terrans were particularly obsessive about pointing out the differences between sentient species while proclaiming we were all equal. Shifting in my chair, I prepared a curt defense. Then I took a long sip of my brandy for liquid courage.

But next, Pappy grew sullen. The light left his eyes,

and a storm seemed to be brewing on the horizon of his leathery brow. "You're not a fan of Terrans, are ye', Ms. Galikor?"

I winced. My overactive facial expressions must have given me away. "I think every one of us has our hypocrisies and biases."

"Aye," Pappy said, studying me. "But you see our foolishness, don't ye'? Cliptorgians are not such a stubborn bunch. I've never met a Cliptorgian who refused to admit when they were wrong, for instance."

Pappy sat there expecting my reply. I was extremely uncomfortable, at a loss for words. When I stammered, giving none, he shifted gears, asking, "Don't you think speech is a sign of an intelligent species?"

Clearly, I was on a different wavelength than this strange old star-rover, for I couldn't connect a single one of his thoughts. I supposed that was due in large part to the fact that he was internalizing most of it. I reassured myself it wasn't me. Nor was it the two sips of brandy at half past noon. No, it was, indeed, the disjointed conversational habits of dear Mr. Artemis Bounty.

"Well?" Pappy took his final swig of whiskey.

Grimtash, what had his question been? 'Is speech a sign of an intelligent species?'

"I would never argue it should be considered the *only* mark of intelligence," I said sternly. Accounting for the number of brainless, entitled pedestrians I had witnessed who seemed *only* to vocalize their selfish needs, I dared not be too hasty with such a sweeping generalization. "But listening to how someone speaks and interacts is an excellent way to gauge their intelligence, at least… to a certain extent," I offered. "So, yes. It is *a* mark of intelligence, but not *the only* mark."

Pappy stared at me. "Is that all, professor," he jabbed. I was unmoved, recognizing his tone as one of harmless play.

"Yes," I said, sipping my brandy. Let him jab.

"Yeah," Pappy said, growing somber suddenly as he stared into his empty glass, perhaps willing the ice to melt faster and provide him with a chaser. "Yeah, that's what I thought." Pappy sucked his next breath in through shuddering lips. "Look, I don't want you to get hurt," he said seriously. "This whole thing, it's all a façade." He gestured with two wagging fingers at the gold crown molding that trimmed the bar's deep green ceiling and walls, then snickered. "A façade charade," he said, raising his arms and wiggling his fingers like the bogey man. He paused, lowered his hands dramatically, then nodded at the crystal chandelier over the bar, burning old fashion filament lightbulbs less than a meter above us. "The lengths we'll go to for luxury, 'ey?"

My mind raced. I could not make heads or tails of the conversation… and I wanted to know how he thought I might get hurt. Or was he just babbling?

The barkeep came over. "Can I get you another," he asked.

"I shouldn't," Pappy muttered to himself.

"I mean, you're gonna' be here a while," I said, holding up my still-full brandy glass.

Selfishly, I needed him to keep talking. Even if I didn't pull any straight answers out of him, maybe I could make sense of what he was saying. I was worried, but I wasn't certain I needed to be.

There had been industry rumors of mechanical challenges while the *Ichthus* was in its testing phase. Perhaps Pappy's station meant he was privy to safety concerns?

"Fair 'nough," he said without a fight as he slid his glass to the boy-tender. "Yessir, I'll have just one more... and lemme' get a water, too."

"Thank you," I offered. The boy smiled appreciatively and poured a fresh glass of water for Pappy first.

"Put it on my tab," Pappy offered, "and add a thirty-percent gratuity for yer'self, lad." As his drinking progressed, so too did the intensity of Pappy's grizzled old sailor drawl. At that point, it was in full swing.

The bartender smiled earnestly and thanked him, then skittered back down the bar to his register, where he no doubt went to make immediate note of Pappy's generous gratuity. Once he was out of earshot, I leaned in. "Before he came over, you said you didn't want me to get hurt," I said quietly, making certain only Pappy could hear me say it. "Am I in danger?"

Pappy stared straight ahead at a neon reptile sign glowing lime green on the wall above the bar's top-shelf liquors. The ghastly grimace that grasped his face haunts me still. He turned, his leathery skin tightening, blanching white as finest ash. All humor and goodwill fled from the corners of his face. "Everyone aboard this ship is in danger. The passengers, the crew… the *captain*. Especially the captain," he said. With that, he lifted his whiskey glass again and tilted it to the sky. There it remained until the entirety of its contents sloshed down his gullet. "Yeah, we're too far in it to turn back now," he said, sighing with resignation. "Unless…"

"Unless what?"

"If you tell our story – write it for all the 'verse to know – then I think I can keep you safe."

"Our story," I questioned, waggling a finger back and forth between the two of us.

"Oh, no, no. There's hardly a story here! Just two lonely souls sharing a drink. I mean no offense… but no. I meant me and my, uh… *crewmates*." Pappy chuckled.

The joke was unclear to me. I said nothing, just watched as he studied the liquid left in his glass. He swished it around a little, took a swig, and set his glass back down with a finite clunk on the bar top. "Aye, you're a clever girl," he said. "I pledge here and now to defend you from what's coming, Ms. Galikor." He removed his floppy bucket hat and placed it over his heart.

There was that strange warning of his again. "What makes you think I need defending?" I wanted to get him back on topic, but in the moment, I couldn't help myself.

Pappy didn't stumble. "Of course, you don't... *of course* you don't! Forgive me, dear." He slapped his hands down on the bar. "Well, I gotta' hit the head, then I should probably sleep this off. I'm on third shift tonight." With that, he pushed off the bar to stand.

"Hell," he added, "I'm on third shift *every* night, now." He turned to leave and toppled to the floor with a sickening thud.

7. WHAT LIES BENEATH

'Aft Deck E'

There was the hallway placard I'd spotted the previous day. Finally, we were close to Pappy's station.

As soon as he had hit the floor, there was no turning back. I knew I had to help him. Besides, something deep down in the cold, logical side of my brain said that, if he was blackout drunk and I was helping him back to his quarters, it gave me the opportunity to poke around. He'd staggered with half his weight rested on me the whole way – we were in our third and final winding hallway, his arm draped over my shoulders as he limped along. My own gait was hobbled by the weight of his load.

Pappy's slack neck snapped up like an agitated goose. "Shiver me timbers, look alive," he slurred. In all my life, I've never heard a person sincerely utter such a cartoonish phrase in earnest, but so help me,

Pappy said exactly that. He was an odd duck, to say the least, and more than a little misplaced in time.

We rounded one final corner, and there at its lonely dead end was Pappy's chair. It was occupied by a young woman. She was Terran, judging by her blond hair. Cliptorgians have no genetics which produce blond hair… not naturally, anyway. And she wore the same dark green coveralls as Pappy. She, however, wore a crisp black chauffeur's cap which must have been a part of the uniform, for its tiny brim was the same emerald green as the coveralls.

She stood watch over the circular hatch in the floor, just as Pappy had been when I found him. I pushed Pappy back against the wall, just out of sight of the young woman. Fortunately, her face was aglow with the light from her datapad, to which her eyes were transfixed. Her index finger occasionally danced up to the screen and tapped something. No doubt she was playing some mindless game.

"Now what," I whispered. "There's someone else on guard."

Pappy wrinkled his nose. "What do they look like?"

"Young Terran woman. Blond." We were both deathly quiet. I was impressed at how Pappy seemed to recover his faculties in that moment.

"That'll be Beth," Pappy said definitively. He tugged my arm, still using me to keep himself steady, and we retreated further. Then, Pappy produced a short-range Com from one of the many pockets in his coveralls and tapped 'Record.' A red light on the Com blinked and Pappy spoke clearly without increasing his volume. "Midshipman B. Sidney, you've been requested on Aft Deck A. I repeat, please report to Aft Deck A." His Com chirped as it transmitted the recording.

Only a few moments later, we could barely hear Pappy's message playing out on Beth's own short-range com. She muttered something before the chair legs squeaked.

"Follow my lead," Pappy said. He dropped to the floor and rolled between two lengths of pipe running along the hallway. I did the same and was instantly doused in inky black shadows. It was mid-afternoon, but Aft Deck E was in night mode. Perhaps an energy-conserving tactic? Whatever the reason, we lurked in the shadows of the piping as Beth hustled right past us, bound for the lifts.

Once she was out of sight, I waited for Pappy to move. He didn't.

"Pappy?"

No response. I waited another moment.

"Pappy?" I reached forward and shook his foot. I heard a snort, as though I'd woken him from a nap.

"Whazzat?" He shook himself and rolled out from between the pipes. "Sorry. I need to get to bed."

"Well, we're close."

Had he just fallen asleep? I didn't bother to press the issue. Instead, I rolled out of my hiding spot and pulled the old man to his feet. I shouldered much of his weight – perhaps because his clever act of sobriety a moment ago had drained all his energy. Reluctantly, I trudged along with lead-footed Pappy until we were back in that dead-end hallway with his now-vacant guard chair. "Okay," I said, "where do we go from here?"

He murmured something unintelligible and handed me his ID card, then pointed out a security console mounted on the wall next to his chair. There seemed to be no consideration of the potential security risk he was taking by allowing a passenger through. He was so far gone he was relying on me for everything. So long as he stayed in automatic until I got him to his bunk, I thought, I might get some answers.

Without hesitation, I waved his ID over the security console. A light on the panel dinged green, and the lock on the hatch behind me whined with an electronic gasp.

A click and a hiss, and the hatch popped free from its frame in the floor. I grabbed the handle and heaved it wide. I waved Pappy forward, but he clung to the wall, his legs wobbly.

"Sailor," I motivated him, "you look like a dirtwalker. Your legs are so wobbly you'd think you hadn't been out of atmos in decades. Now get your act together and march over to this hatch." If ever a brain could shrug, mine did with this attempt. It was worth a shot.

Miraculously, it was right on-brand, and Pappy snapped to. He collected himself and his backbone straightened, pulling his legs in line with it. He marched proudly across the room to me. Then his legs gave out and he hit the floor... again.

"Whoa," I said as quietly as I could manage. "Okay, let me go first." I eased down onto the ladder, my adrenal responses tingling. Despite the humid cloud of steam billowing up out of the hatch around me, I was shivering with excitement. I'd never seen how the Raffe meat was ground into sausage, so to speak.

The foggy engine steam was stifling. There was so much water vapor in the air it made my body reflexively reluctant to take a deep breath. Like the Terran Dante Alighieri, I felt like I was descending into Pappy's inferno. Instead of the molten hue of furnace, however, my own descent was into a dense green bog. I nearly slipped when my feet found the floor, but then my soled toes found a spongy non-skid mat. Sloshing water echoed off metal all around us as our shoes squeaked on the floors. I groped ahead in the fog, unable to see more than half a meter in front of me.

"Cuhrfhl," Pappy warned as he wobbled down the ladder. "Don't fall in my moat." He nodded slackly over his shoulder, and I turned away from the ladder, putting my hands in front of me and moving with precision. It was only four steps to the guardrail, which practically materialized in the steam before my eyes. The dim green overhead lights danced between the layers of fog and the surface of the water. The water itself was an unnatural cobalt, like some toxic sterilization chemical. For as beautiful as the angry blues and mysterious greens were as they played off each other, there was nothing natural about them.

I grew ever so slightly lightheaded, and my vision felt as though it were telescoping, distancing my brain from my body in a narrow and shadowy mind tunnel. As my head swung, images trailed in prismatic impressions. I huffed, forcing the billowing fumes out of my nostrils.

Something moved beneath the surface of the water, and I grabbed the handrail, a wave of dizziness washing over me. Pappy nudged me from behind and I yelped. Somehow, I'd forgotten he was even with me.

"How do you live down here?" I tried whispering my question, but my voice echoed off everything: the metal walls, slippery catwalk, the rippling water. Even the railing seemed to bounce back a frail echo of my voice, plunked in my ear like water droplets in a bucket.

Pappy said nothing, just leaned on me, his eyelids drooping like a sleepwalker. I edged along the railing, waiting for him to keep up. We scuttled forward until the open moat room closed into a narrow hallway, where emerald running lights traced a path ahead through the shroud of steam.

"There's not a lot of illumination down here," I said, more for his sake than my own. The saturated greens and blues made it harder to differentiate anything. There, at the end of the tunnel, was a service window. The wall was white, the window was clear, and the green lights were brighter. Through the glass,

I could see a coffee lounge and, beyond it, three domicile suites. It was much more pleasantly lit in warm yellows and soft whites; the same way a healthy yellow star bathes the rolling hills and craggy canyons of planets near and dear to it.

I swiped Pappy's ID on the security panel outside the door. It bleeped and clicked as the latch released, allowing it to pop open. I swung Pappy's weight over the threshold first, then used our momentum to shuffle him to the nearest couch in the lounge.

"Ugh," he muttered with exhaustion. "Thank ye'. Thank ye' very much, dear."

"Can you manage from here?"

"Yesh," he said, his nod cut short as his head lurched forward and would not budge further, presumably having exerted itself to the fullest already.

"Okay, good," I said. "You just… sleep this off."

With that, I took my leave, and I should confess, Pappy's ID. In truth, it was absent-minded at first. But as I reached the door to leave and felt it in my pocket, I stopped myself from returning it. If I kept it, I told myself, I could check on Pappy later that night. Not only was he dangerously intoxicated and seemingly alone, but I also needed more of his story. I could put together a character profile based on his idiosyncrasies, but I needed more tales about his life serving aboard ships. Maybe there was even enough for a book on Pappy alone: *The Drunken Sailor*, I mused. What can you do? Nonfiction was a big seller.

My mind raced like so as I made it back to the

strange, boggy moat room. The steam billowed everywhere, all the way down the hallway to Pappy's quarters, but the fumes and disorientation lingered only in that belching, sloshing chamber. I held my hands out, they landed on the rail, and I moved along it.

After a few steps, my right hand dragged through a slimy mucous on the railing and I recoiled. It stunk like dried out algae and dead fish. My empty stomach lurched, burning hot with anger at the putrid smells.

I reached the ladder, and the steam cloud wasn't so thick. I realized then that I'd left the hatch open. The cloud of moisture issued upward like the smoke off a stick of incense, racing to its conclusion.

I could see a few yards ahead, and it was then that I noted the scuba gear hanging neatly at the base of the ladder. Did Pappy have to go down into this billowing muck?

I knelt at the water's edge, holding firm to the railing as I peered down into that roiling pool. There, staring back at me, were two glowing yellow orbs. They blinked, then leapt forward, crashing through the surface of the water. A needle-toothed maw and swollen pink gills surged at me as a creature like none I'd ever seen burst forth to challenge me.

Stumbling back, I slipped on the wet metal floor. I caught myself on the exit ladder and hoisted myself back up, squaring my shoulders and balling my hands into fists. Very few Cliptorgian women have a 'flight' response; we are survivors; we will almost always stand our ground to fight. It was a natural reflex.

My attacker belched and roared, grabbing the railing, and pulling itself up onto the deck. Its skin seemed deep green, nearly tar-black, with a brighter face and white stripes that seemed to glow in the unworldly lights all around us. Its frowning mouth and spine-finned back suggested a fish-like evolutionary origin, but the webbed bipedal monster before me stood well over my height. It was also built twice as wide… and stunk of the mucous I'd touched on the handrail.

"Get out," the thing belched, its gills flexing each time it formed a vowel sound.

I did not move. I was stunned. "You… speak?"

The creature did not answer, only roared, flexing its gills until I thought its face might unfurl before my very eyes. It swiped at me with webbed paddle hands that scratched my arm like sandpaper as I dodged the force of the strike. I countered by lunging at its ankles – or finned foot joints – with my own sweeping kick.

That toppled the beast and sent it scrambling. I jumped, skipping the lower rungs of the ladder, and hoisted myself to safety through the hatch. I felt the ladder shake as the beast rammed into it with a clang, desperately trying to reach me.

Without thinking, I rolled over and slammed down the hatch. A howl and a nasty thud from the other side told me I had injured my assailant.

I laid there catching my breath for a moment before sitting up. There, on the floor next to me, was one severed burgundy digit, its ripped webbing oozing with fishy mucous and blood as thick and black as oil.

Without thinking, I snatched it up off the floor. I wrapped it in my pocket square and stuffed it into the inner breast pocket of my waistcoat. I did this all in one fell swoop, then hurried back to my cabin as fast as my trembling legs could carry me.

8. WAITING THINGS OUT

Once safely in my room, I bolted the door, activated the 'Do Not Disturb' status, and rushed over to the writing desk. From there I emptied my pockets, setting down the kerchief with the severed finger, now stained black with alien blood. I produced a few tissues and three spare Digits of currency I had in my pocket, but Pappy's ID was no longer with me. No, I thought, that can't be right. I stood, gently pushing the chair back, and patted myself down.

Nothing.

Where had it gone? I'd left with it – had even felt it in my pocket as I shut the door to Pappy's quarters.

Clearly, I had dropped it, but where? I searched the floor of my quarters. Something thumped against my door, rattling it in its magnatrak frame. I leapt away from it, barely stifling a cry of shock. To the peephole my eye wandered, but all it caught was a shifting shadow dashing amidships.

Oh, no! My mind cried out internally; had I let the beast out? I had and it had surely followed me.

I tried quieting my breath, which I realized was coming in short and ragged gasps. My heart hammered in my chest like an unwanted knock at the door. I took another deep breath and claimed the space around me. Finally, my internal turmoil steadied, lifting the weight off my chest.

My curiosity then persisted. I unlocked my door and deactivated its seal, opting for manual mode so I could crack it open ever so slightly. Unsure if I was alone, I dipped my head out into the hallway slowly. I turned to my left, gazing down the sprawling length of the Deck D hallway. There was no one in sight.

I held my breath, careful not to make a sound. It was harder to hear with my pulse thumping in my ears. Something moved down by the stairwell entrance. I heard the door latch with a heavy metallic click. Only emergency stairwells used old bar-latch hinged doors, I thought. Who had ducked into the emergency stairwell? I stepped out into the hallway, then decided it wasn't my business. I was already on edge; I didn't need to go chasing noises. I needed to stay focused on Pappy's ID.

I scanned the carpeted floor, retracing my path down the hall in my mind as I searched the carpet with my eyes.

No trace of Pappy's ID anywhere. Zirkrum, I thought. There goes my free pass. I decided it was worth retracing my steps as far as Aft Deck E. If the wrong person got a hold of Pappy's ID, he might get in trouble. It would be hard not to feel responsible should that come to pass.

Forty minutes later, I returned to my cabin empty-handed. I hadn't dared go all the way to the hatch, but I had gotten as far as the placard, only one corner away from that awful hole in the floor.

Coward, I scolded myself as I activated the panel to my quarters and slipped back inside. For all I knew that ID was lying on the floor right next to that terrible hatch. I had, after all, been jostled when the creature tried to escape.

What harm could have come from poking my nose around the corner?

I locked myself in once more, retreating to the writing desk. Without the ID, I reasoned, I could not return to Pappy. I would have to wait until he sobered up and sought me out. Or perhaps I could track him down once he was back at his post. He'd mentioned third shift. If he did not come to see me by the twenty-third hour that night, I would seek him out at his frightful trapdoor once his shift started. After all the nonsense of the afternoon, it was now creeping on hour seventeen in the standard cycle.

First, I set about recording every detail and recollection, ran the transcription on my conversation at the bar with Pappy, then I unwrapped the kerchief and studied my catch.

The beast had been rough to the touch, a granular scratching sensation that left a brush burn on my left arm where it swiped at me. Though the beast had seemed as black as squid ink in the strange green light of the moat room, I could see now that its finger was of the finest rich dark burgundy, mottled with tiny speckles of brightest sunburst orange and pearly white, all concentrated around the finger pads. A tattered string of membrane dangled from the specimen, and from its scrappy remains I could see in the light that it was indeed translucent, but only the slightest bit.

Given the observations I'd made, albeit briefly and under heightened adrenal response, I deduced that my attacker had been aquatic or perhaps amphibious. I had observed gills, but I had not expected its full frame to be that of an upright biped. Flippers or no, I could not deny the form I'd seen crashing out of the water: jointed legs, jointed flipper feet, arms with flippered hands... hands with fingers.

Next my attention was drawn to the fingernail... or rather the claw... at the very least, it was a little needle-like spine. Yes, that was it, I thought turning the specimen over and looking at it in profile. Most importantly, I could see the bone. These creatures had a skeletal structure. Feeling brave, I used the surface of the desk to check the pliability of the needlelike claw. It bent so much, expressed so much malleability, that I thought it might not bend back into shape. But it did after a time, driving me to the conclusion that it was of a cartilaginous nature.

I had dinner ordered to my room.

Time crept by slowly.

I re-read my notes: added to them as necessary.

When room service knocked on my door with dinner, I wrapped my specimen up in the already-stained handkerchief and tucked it safely in my breast pocket. Room service wheeled a cart in for me and I ate dinner right on the trolly, in front of my porthole window. I wish I could say that I enjoyed my view of the stars as their light travelled millions of years to wink at me, but I did not. Every star reminded me of those disturbing, glinting eyes. Every streak of hot white light from meteorites reminded me of those needled teeth in those flaring, fishy jowls.

"Get out," they'd bark in my memory, and I'd bury my gaze in my soup. Halfway through this eating ritual from a disturbed mind, the lights in my room flickered, and the climate control sputtered.

I took a sip to wait it out.

Again, the power faltered and then failed completely. I was plunged into darkness before the orange emergency running light ticked on over the door. It made the hallway and adjoining bathroom look like a room ablaze, doused in that fiery orange warning.

The loudspeaker system clicked on with a crackle. The speaker was mounted over the door, in the same fixture as the emergency light. The calm paternal voice of Captain Englehorn reached out from somewhere else onboard. "Attention passengers: this is your captain speaking. It appears we're experiencing a malfunction–"

Near him, another Com line crackled. The person on the other end was screaming for help. Quickly, the feed was cut and someone in the cockpit muttered a Terran cuss.

"Shouldn't be anything to worry about, just a momentary power failure. All life support systems are run by auxiliary functions, so all is well here. We'll be up and running again shortly. We'll keep you posted."

The Com clicked off. I sat there, paralyzed as I tried to process what I'd just heard.

I cannot say if I sat there for ten seconds or ten minutes, but I sat in that moment a good long while. What was going on?

Finally, I checked my clock. It was 22:02. Later than I was expecting. How long had I sat there considering every possible and extreme outcome?

There was a furious knock on my door. I jumped with a start, but I stayed quiet as I slinked over to the peephole. As I crept close, I held my breath. A quick check of the light told me no shadow would obscure the peephole should I venture to see who was there. I might not answer, depending on who or what I saw. And I had every right, I encouraged myself.

It was Pappy.

I was surprised to see him standing up straight and dressed smart in a clean uniform. He hadn't shaved, so his stubble was threatening to blossom into a short beard, and the bags under his eyes drooped like sacks of grain, but I could hardly fault him, having seen his condition less than eight hours ago.

Relief flooded my chest as I let out a sigh. Standing up straight, I unlocked the door and let it slide open.

Then, I ushered him inside.

Before I could press the button to close the door again, a fishy flipper wedged itself in the track, trapping the door in its place.

9. MUTINY OR DEATH

July 8ᵗʰ, A.D. 2299
22:23 IST

In a flurry of water and mucus, five fishy beasts forced their way into my quarters. Pappy entered behind them. He checked down the hallway to make sure no one had seen and shut the door, turning his back to it.

My nose warned that, though no one had seen them, there was a good chance someone may still smell them. Each of the fish people was armed with a sword, fire axe or meat cleaver. I noted shock-sticks on two of them, holstered at the hip. Out of water, they all seemed coated in a clear, slimy membrane, like that which I had found on the railing. I also noted that the most impressive specimen among them in both size and physique had a bandaged left hand. Inky blood had seeped through and stained the cloth where the big thing's index finger should have been.

Unwittingly, I placed my hand on my breast pocket, where I had stowed its severed finger. "Varaan kuhl," I cussed in my native tongue. "Pappy, what is this?"

"Give thy thoughts no tongue," the big fish barked at me. I tried not to scoff in disbelief. What pomp – what pretension was this?

"Bowsprit, Mizzenmast: search her," the big thing growled next. The two fishy mates with shock-sticks hustled forward. They groped at me until one of them landed on my inner breast pocket. With an air of annoyance, I swatted the thing's flipper away.

"In my culture, it's inappropriate to touch people like that," I said firmly.

The thing called Bowsprit recoiled at my touch, squawking as its crown of spines pricked up and its gills flared. It looked at the leader... the big one... and bowed.

"Sir," the beast squawked, "I wish not to offend Professor's ally, but she beholds a lump in her pocket."

The big one sneered. "Remove the lump from your pocket, if ye' truly be an ally to our Pappy," the big thing barked at me.

Pappy caught my eye, gave his head the slightest nod, tried to sooth me with the twinkle in his eyes. I was unaffected, but I was overwhelmed and, frankly, eager to move things along. If the monster condemned me for taking its finger, so be it. Producing the handkerchief, I marched the few steps across my cabin floor to the monster and slapped the stained handkerchief in his palm.

"I retained that," I said haughtily, "when you attacked me by the moat." I had no idea what or who I was dealing with, but for some reason the whole situation had me growing hot under the collar.

The big brutish fish plucked at the kerchief, which came unspooling, and the severed finger dropped to the floor. Every fish minion in the room gasped in horror. Pappy groaned.

"What'd you do that for," the old man complained at me.

"Pappy, I was helping you back to your room," I pleaded for him to defend me.

"You shouldn'ta' been down there in the first place," he scolded.

My back straightened as my heart grew indignant. He had been blackout drunk. He wouldn't have even made it to his hatch without my help. "I was following your drunken instructions," I lied… convincingly, I might add. "You needed my help getting back to your quarters."

That broke his mounting ire. His brow lifted, shriveling with consideration. "I did overdo it on the whiskey, Dread," he said, turning to the big fish.

"Do you even care," roared the fish Pappy called Dread. "My finger bobbles about the ground, maimed by a stranger, and you pander to her because she's your fellow ape? Fucking hairballs, all of you!" The brutish Dread stomped like a toddler to emphasize his insult.

"What have we said about the language," Pappy scorned like some disapproving aunt.

"Do not correct me!" Dread whirled around in his spot. He wore a makeshift cape of some ragged royal purple fabric. It dripped with water and fish mucus. "I am free to talk as I please now!" He pulled a worn mallet from his belt and raised it like a scepter. I saw that it had a bronze metal handle, and barnacles of every color grew freely from its worn rubber club. The reek of salt water washed through my room in waves as he swung his arm. Instantly I switched to breathing through my mouth. Nothing like a bad smell to make one lose composure in a high-stress situation. At least, my sensitive pallet thought so.

"You," Dread swung his little club so it was pointed at me. I was processing the fact that Pappy felt free to scold this hulking beast. There was something parental about it.

"What," I asked, keeping my back straight so as not to shrink to his challenge. When encountering any new species, one must be hyperaware of their posturing and presence. To get distressed or shrink up at a time like this would only display signs of weakness to my opposition. I could not come across as inferior, not even on a subconscious level.

"Pappy says you are a scribe?"

"Yes," I said slowly and surely.

"Ah," the big creature sighed. "My tongue will tell the anger of my heart, or else my heart concealing it will break."

Pappy raised his hand. "Eh heh, that's Shakespeare. I taught him that. He's a big fan of Shakespeare."

Oh good, I chided internally. A tyrant with a taste for literature. Instead, I nodded and smiled but said nothing. Frankly, I wasn't sure what to say. I had so many questions… the least of which was 'Pappy taught this thing Shakespeare?' However, I decided to allow for more open-ended elaboration on what exactly they were up to. "Those are ancient, powerful words. What anger sits in your heart?" I daresay my tone played into his noble melodrama.

"My people have been wronged., and today, we claim retribution. I would have a great scribe to record our conquest."

"Conquest…" I pondered. The power outage?

"Without the labor of my shiver, the great prison tank *Ichthus* will faulter. We are your power! We are your ingenuity, you filthy beasts!"

"Dreadnought," Pappy scolded, butting in. "We mustn't take our aggression out on Telfera. Also, she's not Terran. The people who own *Ichthus* are Terrans. Telfera is Cliptorgian."

The beast sniffed the air, taking two steps closer as he did and looking me up and down as his flaring nostrils waggled my way.

"She smells of mammal."

"Yes. Cliptorgians are also mammals. But they're very different. Remember your lessons?"

I was listening to them, trying to gather what I

could from context clues, but the survivalist in me was already making moves of her own. The fish thing was called Dreadnought, and he was leading a... a conquest of the starship? The cape and scepter made it clear he fancied himself a ruler or leader of some kind. And Pappy... the quirky old sailor I thought I might biograph, was teaching him.

The beast squared his shoulders and bowed to me. As he raised himself up and our eyes met again, he spoke. "I frightened you even after I observed you aiding my professor," Dreadnought gestured with a webbed hand to Pappy.

Professor, I noted with some confusion.

"I should have assumed you were an ally and left you alone. I was shamed for my actions when you severed my finger. You have claimed a piece of me in battle. As our traditions demand, I cannot force you to join my shiver."

Though I was unsure what a 'shiver' was, he gestured to the other fish people in the room. I assumed that was their word for pack or school.

"However, a great new dawn is upon us, and we would like to request your services as the scribe of our harrowing revolution!"

The other fish clicked their teeth, chattering in agreement. It was an eerie, delicate clacking sound that very nearly mimicked applause.

"We are breaking free from the tanks of *Ichthus*," Dreadnought proclaimed, "and founding our own kingdom!"

Pappy removed his hat, placing it over his heart as he addressed me like some national hero. "As an educated traveler, and as a professional writer, your account of Dreadnought's people and our situation here would go a long way towards helping them establish political autonomy."

"What if I decline," I asked. Selfishly, I admit I wanted the story. In that moment, it became clear that Pappy was merely a supporting role. The real story was this strange new alien species. In my lap was a chance to record the first known interactions with a new form of biological consciousness.

Nonfiction sells. I wanted to write bigger things. I had no idea what their mission would entail, and my resistance was a mere ploy for more information. I didn't get much.

"If you decline, my people will leave you here in your quarters. You will not journey forth to the bridge with us, and therefore, you will certainly perish when we purge the ship of air-suckers. Please understand this is not personal, it is merely a part of the plan. Thank you for your consideration."

Dreadnought bowed again stiffly and stepped back against the wall. All those glowing eyes stared at me, some flame yellow, others blue as ice. They glared at me from the harsh shadows of the orange emergency light in my cabin.

I processed everything as quickly as I could. Shock of some kind was setting in, for my limbs felt numb and distant, as though all my physical energy was concentrated in my skull – my brain – on this one crucial decision. Dreadnought was leading a mutiny. I could join him – go with Pappy – and hope they succeeded, or I could sit here and wait to die.

"I do not mean to offend... or to insult. I merely wish to clarify something with... your highness." I tried to make myself sound like a proper subject, even stooping to curtsey the slightest bit when I posed my disclaimer.

Dreadnought raised his barnacled mallet up to the ceiling, as if summoning some holy spirit into the tool. His instrument of divine right, perhaps? "Ask away, my dear, ask away," he said with gaiety in his voice.

"If I record your overthrow here, you realize of course that you will have to be willing to let me go at some point?"

Dreadnought's next breath seemed to stagger in through only one of his little nostrils.

"Er, not that I should wish to leave your court, except that I must in order to tell the tale... the tale of your conquest aboard the *Starship Ichthus*!"

The hulking, neckless, barrel-chested brute sighed. He nibbled on his mallet as he thought things through. "I like survivalists," he growled at me as he nodded with approval. "We are all survivalists, are we not," he said, rallying his troops to stomp their stumpy flippered feet on the carpet and hoot and gurgle like horny toads. The smell their chirruping stirred was of the most putrid sulfur, and I could not help but note the excess mucus their gills seeped forth as they sang. I drew my breath in through my mouth to avoid the smell, but instead I could taste the air I was breathing… their air.

My mind raced with questions as I considered my options for survival. What would happen if their mutiny failed? What would I get for throwing in with this lot? More importantly, where were the lifeboats from here? I hadn't seen any. Surely, they were around. The only way to find out, I reasoned, was to stay alive. That's what I deserved for sniffing out a story, a life-or-death scenario with a hitherto unknown form of intelligent life. To this day, I don't know how much I did it for survival, and how much I did it for the story… but I accepted Dreadnought's offer on the spot.

"I'll join you," I said. "I'll take any oath you like, and I'll write about what it is you're doing here."

"You please me," Dreadnought grumbled. "We push on!"

I sighed as they ushered me out of my room and around the corner, to the shadows of the maintenance stairwell. So, it was mutiny then…

10. KOMEOPIANS

July 9ᵗʰ, A.D. 2299
00:13 IST

It was after midnight as we marched in darkness to the Operations Deck. Dreadnought kept checking over his shoulder to make sure I was within earshot. We did not take the passenger thoroughfares, but rather several maintenance ducts and stairwells that led up. It was much like my walk with Graves to the Command Bridge.

I figured I should start with basics since I couldn't keep calling them 'fish people.' So, as we cleared my hallway into the first stairwell I politely asked. "What do your people call themselves?"

"We are Kō-mē-Ōp-iǝn," Dreadnought belched. "Our Mother Ocean is the Great Koh. We... are refugees."

Pappy leaned over and showed me the spelling of

these new words by writing them out on his hand with a ballpoint pen. 'Komeopian' and 'Koh' were how Pappy had translated the sounds into our modern tongue like some amateur transonuscribe[14].

"What are you taking refuge from," I asked. It seemed like the easiest course of questioning. I quite forgot I was mutinying at all. For the moment, this was just a curious interview.

Dreadnought stopped at the next landing and stared at me. He was truly massive – at least twice as wide as me and clearly built bigger than the others of his species. No wonder they kowtowed at his every exhale. He was terrifying.

"We fled our home world," he growled, "for we were no longer welcome to share her vast oceans with our kind. Then your people found us."

"She's not Terran," Pappy corrected him.

Dreadnought stopped, glowering at Pappy. He leaned close to my forehead and bared his teeth. With the most unpleasant flicker of his mouth, he sniffed me.

"Still stinks like ape glands," he said with a defiant look to Pappy. "So, you're from the purple world. Clup–" Dreadnought hesitated.

"Try it," Pappy encouraged.

---

[14] A highly specialized linguist who translates and transcribes vocalizations across alien languages. This profession grew from necessity during the early days of the Clipto-Terran Alliance, circa 2142. Notably, the title was created by Arvessa Grimmol, the Cliptorgian translator who oversaw writing that treaty.

"Clupt–" Dreadnought tried again but then got aggravated and swatted blindly at the air. "I cannot form the sounds!"

"Clip-*tohr*-gē-uh," Pappy encouraged.

A new group of Komeopians was moving up the stairs, their webbed feet smacking on the cool metal. There were four in all, their markings difficult to pick out in the low, blue nighttime running lights. I saw Dreadnought puff out his chest.

"ENOUGH," he roared demonstrably. "I've had my fill learning about your cultures, old man. Now she learns of ours. Our species has a history equally rich!"

With that, he pushed Pappy aside. As Pappy was shuffled out of the way, we caught each other's eye for just a moment. For a millisecond, I saw his uncertainty as he flashed me a meager smile. I had the distinct sense that Pappy had once been in control of this situation, though he clearly no longer was.

The Komeopian newcomers finished their ascent, and all but one of them waited on the landing below ours. The one who hustled the rest of the way up to us was clearly leading their group. He hustled up the stairs to us.

Dreadnought smiled as the newcomer approached. "Spar, you're early," he said, gurgling in a way that I assume meant he was pleased.

Spar flexed his spikes and gills, a gesture the Komeopians seemed to be using as a form of military salute. "Aye, sir. Our job is done," said Spar.

Dreadnought nodded. "Good." He turned back to

his own group. "Boatswain," he bellowed.

From behind us, the tallest, leanest of Dreadnought's disciples stepped forward. "We begin phase two. Go rendezvous with Team Fleg. Have them prepare for the flood."

"Aye, sir," Boatswain saluted by extending the spiny fins at the back of his head. He stayed back as the rest of us climbed one final flight of stairs.

"What are you flooding," I asked. Dreadnought either didn't hear me or didn't care to acknowledge. Either way, he rumbled up the staircase away from me, his bare wet flippered feet smacking the metal as he went.

The next landing seemed to be the last; we were at the top of the stairwell. Dreadnought wheeled around and hissed for silence. "You!" He pointed at me.

"Yes," I said, still not willing to be intimidated by Dreadnought's blustering. I had seen such behavior, in Terran men especially… and the lower tier apes that still beat their chests in the depths of Earth's few remaining forest preserves.

"You will wait here with Kelp." As he said this, a meager little Komeopian squeezed through the others and tipped its fins in salute.

"Kelp," Dreadnought hissed, "keep her here at all costs. If she makes to run away, you may lay your eggs in her."

"What," I sputtered. There was no positive way to interpret that.

"You'll be alright," Pappy whispered reassuringly,

patting Kelp's back like a loyal puppy while flashing me an encouraging smile. "Just stay put. Kelp is really a very gentle soul."

Like a loyal puppy, Kelp spread his toothy maw in an almost comical grin, bobbing his head up and down in agreement. As he did, his tongue lolled out of the side of his mouth ever so slightly, waggling between his hooked, needle-like teeth.

"Silence," Dreadnought commanded, clicking his teeth. "Komeopians… arm yourselves!"

His shiver, now eight aliens strong, held up their clubs and blades to their leader. They waggled them in the air, and Dreadnought reached his big fat fin for Pappy. The flipper-like fingers made a wet sopping sound as they slapped Pappy on the shoulder.

"Showtime, Professor," he said as he pushed the old man forward, towards the solitary hatch door on the landing ahead of us. As Pappy was ushered forward, his encouraging half-smile quickly shrank into an uncertain grimace.

Kelp, my meager new chaperone, tugged me gently back down a few stairs, offering more space for the others to get around us both.

Once all nine of them were past, they shut the hatch behind them. The thick metal door muted the surprised shouts of Terrans reacting to Dreadnought and his intruders.

Despite the ruckus, the stout Kelp did nothing more than blink at me. His eyelids seemed always to work one at a time. The effect was a glazed, demur look that loitered on the short Komeopian's face. Suspecting my guard might unwittingly overshare, I decided to continue my reconnaissance.

"Your Dreadnought said you could lay your eggs in me," I tried cautiously. "Is that an expression your people have?"

Kelp blinked again: first the left eye, then the right. He thought hard for a moment longer, then, through his spiked tooth underbite, he said, "Yes."

I nodded, raising an eyebrow, expecting more. Kelp simply breathed heavily and stared at his feet.

"And what does that expression mean?"

"It mean… if run you do… Kelp lay eggs in your chest!" His words were slow and hard to form. They also horrified me.

Had that been a *literal* permissory statement?

A shriek of agony cracked the silent thrum of the ship, echoing through the stairwell. It was coming from the other side of the door. It was Terran.

I spied the placard next to the door, which read 'Aft Operations Deck: Security Barracks.'

Grimtash! They were slaughtering the ship's security force first. All I could do was listen.

Blades clashed, metal slinking and clanging against more metal. In a few instances, metal found meat, the clang terminating with a disgusting wet smack and a shrill, animal howl.

A crackle of electricity erupted inside the security barracks, and a burst of bluish-white light traced the seams around the closed door before me. The thumping and clanging of a life-or-death tussle continued as I stood paralyzed, unable even to back away from those terrible sounds.

I was unsure what else to say to my guard and unwilling to pull focus from the sounds of Dreadnought's fight unfolding just one room away. Two blood-curdling wails, a moan, and a stomping foot later, all was thankfully quiet.

The hatch door lurched open finally as relative silence crept back to us. A dark green Komeopian about my same height, which was just shy of two meters, held the hatch open and faced us. He sneered at me. As our eyes locked, the creature's frosty blue pupils flashed with recognition.

Those eyes, I thought. I'd seen them earlier… in the tank at the Reception Hall. This creature had been the owner of those cold eyes. Yes, I thought. I could see now how the spines on his head seemed to form a crown-like shape. He'd been in the tanks, watching the passengers during boarding procedures. Interesting, I thought. I said nothing.

"Have we victory, Gunwale?" Kelp was eager for news.

"Victory is ours," the one called Gunwale hissed at us. Kelp giggled and clapped gleefully. "Come," Gunwale continued, "Dreadnought has commanded that we each choose a vassal."

Kelp wrapped a slimy, spindly flipper around my wrist and bounded through the door, dragging me with surprising certainty and force. He let go once we were inside, and the hatch snapped shut behind us.

The Komeopians had dismantled and killed the bulk of the ship's security battalion. There were usually twelve to eighteen specialized armed guards in charge of security on a vessel like *Ichthus*. I counted thirteen corpses, and my heart sank. That battalion of security officers would have been our best hope in resisting Dreadnought's usurpation. There was no telling if the Komeopians had killed all but one security officer, or if there were five more elsewhere aboard. Even if there were five more security officers, they were unlikely to all be in one place. Chances were, they'd been called off in pairs to provide an imposing force for any customer service specialist dealing with passenger disputes. It was a common conflict-resolution tactic employed on nearly every cruise I'd taken.

The subordinate security precincts onboard were more like local law enforcement bureaucrats than they were soldiers. They were called 'Accommodation Specialists' – data-pushers and detectives who monitored security feeds, reported petty thefts, and interrogated unruly passengers detained by the ship's security officers. They certainly were not experienced enough to use firearms aboard a starliner, a concept so dangerous, it was a hot topic for political debates. Should firearms of any kind be used aboard spaceships, given the high security risks and the number of accidental deaths it caused each year? I wasn't sure what would be worse: having these awful creatures lay eggs in my chest or being sucked out into space through a hole the size of a bullet. I shook such anxious thoughts from my mind.

Kelp let go of me and staggered forward, crouching over one of the deceased. I noticed all the Komeopians were doing this. They watched Dreadnought, who I could not see at the other end of the room. My view was obscured by his eager disciples. He was kneeling over something. Then, as he ducked his head, I gasped.

Every Komeopian ducked after him, diving their jagged, tusk-like lower teeth into the base of their chosen cadaver's neck, like some vicious tracheotomy. I averted my eyes as I realized Kelp was prying wide those fleshy holes to make his incision larger. Then, unhinging his jaw in a most unnatural way, Kelp extended two long fleshy tubes from under his tongue. As his chest heaved, I saw orbs working through the fleshy tubes, inserted into the corpse through the tracheotomy holes. What in The Rings[15] was I witnessing?

Pappy sauntered over, slinking from a shadowy corner. Perhaps it was just me, but I detected a sinister shift in his demeanor. "Poetic, isn't it?"

Pappy waited a tick, then, when I didn't respond, he added, "Just one of us dies, and it gives several of

---

[15] This Cliptorgian phrase is often used as one might question fate or conjure a deity (e.g. 'What in God's name?') Its origins can be traced back to the dawn of Cliptorgian evolution, where the first recorded religion in the planet's history praised the planet's rings, which provided light to forage by at night.

them life."

"That's an optimistic way of viewing sentient parasitic lifeforms," I muttered.

"I think the Komeopians could use a little optimism," said Pappy, his tone protective and paternal.

It instantly annoyed me, and sardonically I replied, "Really? Based on this display, I'd say a night at the morgue would be far more... reproductive."

The sweet tang of bile stung my nostrils, drifting through the air around me, and I shielded my face. The Komeopians were regurgitating mucus, using it to seal off the tracheotomy holes, encasing the clavicles of their egg-sack corpses in a dripping breastplate of goo. The smell alone was nauseating. I averted my eyes and suppressed the sounds as best I could.

"They can't help the way nature designed them," Pappy scolded. "And you're only seeing their half of the story so far."

"Well, what exactly is the other half, as you understand it?" Without getting hostile, I stared him down and waited.

"Utter disregard and abuse," said Pappy. "From the descriptions I've gathered, they were encountered by merchants and tranquilized like animals. The side effects they described, including memory loss surrounding the event, suggest they were drugged and kidnapped. Does that sound fair to you?"

"No," I said curtly. I could at least agree with him on that.

"I was working this vessel three whole weeks before I realized they were aboard. Security officers and deck officers would come to see me, I'd open the hatch, they'd go down in the tank, and I'd shut the door again." He shook his head, his body heavy with shame. "They were down there to punish Dread and the others. Had them all slaving away at the engines, in scalding hot water and all sorts of pollutants. Their number one cause of death aboard *Ichthus* has been something they call Gill Clot. From what I can figure, callouses develop inside the tissue of their gills because of the pollutants they're breathing in. If they don't catch it or if it spreads too fast, that's it. They eventually lose the ability to breathe underwater. I watched a few of them drown that way... right in front of me. That's when I said, 'No more. These poor things are being forced to serve us. How can I do something to serve them?'"

"How noble of you," I said plainly. It took all of my being not to use the sarcasm I intended. "So, you educated them in all the finer things, like classic Terran literature," I said. "How's that serving your pets?"

Pappy scoffed. "That literature is the mark of a good education. They're *cultured.*"

And yet, I thought without saying a word, if it's taught by a mentor who doesn't fully understand its meaning, how well-educated is the pupil in all actuality?

"Hell," Pappy went on proudly, removing his bucket cap and knocking some dust out of it, "I made sure they had a better education than I did. We barely covered that stuff when I was in school, and when we did, I sure as hell wasn't paying attention." He looked proudly across the room at Dreadnought. "That lad," he said, "is a far better student than I ever was. So, I taught him the stuff I wish I knew. I should've known he'd be leading some day."

"And you're sure *that's* the best role for him? I mean, from what I've seen so far, he seems prone to anger quickly, and he used very little scrutiny before deciding I was trustworthy enough to bring along…"

"Are you suggestin' you *ain't* trustworthy, Ms. Galikor?" Pappy narrowed his gaze, his old grey-blue eyes locking with mine. His right hand dropped to his waist, where he'd holstered a shock-stick.

I went rigid, standing up to my full height. "Not at all," I said firmly. "It was merely an observation: a philosophical consideration."

Pappy was unfazed. "I'm no philosopher," he said with a shrug.

"Then what qualifies you to mentor these beings?" I fired back quickly, for my retort was conceived in reflex.

Pappy's head bobbed up and down impatiently. "I was the only one good enough to care about them. 'Love all, trust a few; Do wrong to none.'" Then, proudly, he added, "That's *All's Well That Ends Well."*

I blinked, processing the quote. "I don't think that answers my question."

"You'll see," was all he said in reply. With that, he turned away, uninterested in my camaraderie. I watched him cross the room and help one of the Komeopians understand how to use the shock-sticks they were picking up off security officers around the room.

So, these were my captors. A madman and his dreadful parasitic pets. I would have rather taken a trip to one of Earth's major cities, where any mammal is guaranteed to catch bed bugs or some damned disease from a displaced, unhinged Terran. Sure, it was inconvenient and mind-numbing, but at least those problems had antidotes. I was feeling more and more convinced that my current condition did not...

11. THE RUNT OF THE SHIVER

As the Komeopians chortled mucus, I knelt to re-strap my sandals. It was then that I spotted an ankle pistol under one of the benches which lined a wall of changing lockers. Pappy had moved on and was searching through a cache of more devious weapons several meters away.

No one was watching me.

Despite my better judgement, I took the pistol. Remaining unarmed was out of the question; if I were going to die on principle, I wouldn't have accepted Dreadnought's offer, I reasoned. Quickly, methodically, I checked the cartridge and put the safety on. Thank the Rings for grandma's homestead.

I turned away from the group to slip the weapon into my tunic, tucking it snuggly into the elastic of my undergarments just below my left armpit. Having already corrected them for groping my chest, I hoped the Komeopians would not notice the concealed weapon until the opportune moment. I wasn't quite sure what that even meant, I just knew I had to wait. The moment would reveal itself to me, I told myself.

To avoid further suspicion, I sidled up next to Pappy.

"No doubt this was *your* strategy." I raised an eyebrow at him.

"How do you mean," he asked without blinking.

"I know what's what. The other security details onboard ships like this are for passenger administration. Petty theft, vandalism, things like that. But this," I extended my arm out to the room, "this is what the captains call their 'Top-Shelf Security.' We're just aft of the Command Bridge now, with no one to stop you. You've condemned your superiors!"

At my utterance of the word 'superiors,' the Komeopians all chortled in tones of shock or disapproval. The great Dreadnought balked nonverbally. As he did, the protuberances around his face flexed, spreading wide and flapping like a kite in an ocean breeze. It was a sharp, disturbing display of spikes and fins and scaley flesh.

Dreadnought practically galloped across the room until he was towering in front of me. I had to lean back to meet his glaring gaze. "What was that word," he challenged. His big belly heaved under the strange slimy vest he wore. Again, I stood my ground as reflexive instinct drove me to.

"I was referring to Pappy's workplace superiors,"

110

I said plainly.

As Dreadnought's angry maw lunged at me, it was hard not to flinch. The stench of his breath was like a belch of foul sea air.

"*Who* is superior," Dreadnought roared. Another hot gust of putrid sea stink washed over me as he asked.

"The only person I report to is Dreadnought," Pappy affirmed, thumbing at the Komeopian with his left hand. He was trying to mitigate their leader's temper. I was not about to make it easy on him. Not now, with the horrible truth before me.

"*No one* is superior to me," Dreadnought barked. "Look around you," he gestured to the fertilized corpses of the ship's security detail. "Do you doubt that nature bestowed us with a superior design?"

"I doubt a good many things, having seen you all... *propagate*," I started. I wanted to leave it at that, but I knew I couldn't. Not if I wanted to live. "However, I will not deny the... *efficacy* of your lifecycle."

"It is poetry," Dreadnought corrected.

"It is efficacy," I insisted. "Particularly if all of these eggs are expected to hatch."

At that, Dreadnought seemed to shrink. His shoulders drooped, and he did not seem as mountainously tall. "They will not all hatch," he said quietly. "It is... a thing of nature," he added somberly.

He turned his back to me, facing the room... facing his comrades. "The next generation of fighters is seeded," he proclaimed. "Now, it is time!"

The Komeopians raised their weapons to the sky and chortled, clicking their teeth at one another in celebration. Dreadnought nodded to Pappy. "Send the signal to Boatswain."

Pappy pulled out a little two-way Com and pressed a shining blue button to transmit. The device chirruped, ready to receive his message. "Boatswain, kill the stack," was all he said. A moment later, the device dinged, and its tiny speaker played a Komeopian voice back to the room.

"Aye, aye!"

At this, the Komeopians all pushed to the front of the barracks, where a heavily armored airlock door dominated the forward wall.

"Sir," cried one of his soldiers at the front of the room.

"What is it, Bowsprit?" Dreadnought peered over the others, trying to see Bowsprit at the front of the room. Everyone cleared a path for him.

"We need 'security clearance' to operate the armored doors," Bowsprit said as Dreadnought joined him at the security console mounted in the wall. I recognized Bowsprit, for I had swatted his hand away when they searched me in my cabin. I made a note that he was of a sturdy build, the same burgundy color as Dreadnaught, and had splashes of yellow scales along his back and on top of his head. It gave the impression of a sailor in a crimson uniform with a long blond ponytail.

"He's right," Pappy said, pushing gently past me and several Komeopians to get closer to Dreadnought again.

"Not a problem," Dreadnought said reassuringly. "Examine the dead," he instructed. "Find me the highest-ranking corpse in the room, and I'll increase your rank among us!"

His minions scurried about the dimly lit room. Everything aboard was in night mode. I found a clock readout: 00:42 IST. I made a note in my datapad, resolving then to try to record each criminal act these *monsters* committed. Perhaps then my notes, complete with timestamps, could prove useful evidence.

The Komeopians of Dreadnought's shiver chattered and clicked teeth as they compared the ID badges on each corpse. As they went about it, an exchange in the corner drew my attention. Kelp was speaking their native, gurgling, sing-song tongue. By now, I recognized my guard from earlier as the slightest and least articulate of their fishy crew. Kelp yanked the ID off the corpse nearest him. The elastic lanyard snapped free from its deceased owner, and the crack echoed through the room.

Dreadnought wheeled around to discern the source, and when he saw Kelp standing there with the broken lanyard, he balled his webbed hands into fists and howled with rage. Kelp froze on the spot, shivering and quaking in his lord's shadow. Before anything was spoken, Dreadnought roared, swinging a massive right hook. Out of the corner of my eye, I saw

Pappy lurch forward as a faint gasp of, "No," fluttered from his lips. At the last moment, Dreadnought opened his fist and clobbered Kelp with a wet and thunderous smack.

We all cringed as Kelp yelped like a spanked dog, and the poor creature went tumbling into an open locker in the corner of the room. Even though he emerged again blinking, and even though he spat out two of his pointed teeth, the room knew Dreadnought had spared him by opening his hand. I suppressed a shudder as I imagined what injuries a closed fist might have caused poor Kelp.

Creeping forward, Pappy raised a trembling index finger as he squeaked out a gentle reprimand. "Dread, get a hold of your temper!"

It seemed at that moment, with Pappy methodically inching toward Dreadnought, that he almost meant to slip himself in front of Kelp like a mother trying to shield her child. Curious. He continued, "Members of our shiver are our comrades. There's no need to abuse–"

"*Our* shiver," Dreadnought wheeled, puffing his chest out at Pappy and roaring. "OUR shiver?" He recoiled, sneering. "No, Professor: *my* shiver. You are here because I say you are here. I allow you to be here. You do not know what it is to be Komeopian. You can never know. This is how it is; this is how it has always been. I will instruct my shiver as I see fit."

Pappy stepped back into the shadows, his head hanging low.

Dreadnought turned back toward Kelp. "Do not remove IDs from the bodies," Dreadnought shouted, his tone demonstrative. He leaned over to Kelp as though he were sharing ancient wisdom. "Do you not remember my planning? We may need to use a fingerprint or pupil scan, and we need to keep bodies matched with IDs."

Woozily, Kelp offered the ID back to Dreadnought, who scooped the broken lanyard up in his enormous hand. "This," Dreadnought said, peering at the ID before shoving it in Kelp's face, "says 'ensign.' Do you know what that means?"

Kelp gurgled, working his jaws as he thought. Finally, he shook his head. "Kelp not knows."

"It means he is a pissant! He was at the bottom of the barrel. The runt of the shiver; the omega man. Like you, Kelp!" Dreadnought threw his head back and laughed maniacally.

All the other Komeopians mimicked the mannerisms of their powerful leader. I could not help but feel bad as Kelp blinked pitifully in the corner. I wasn't entirely sure the poor thing realized exactly what was being said. Though, I reminded myself, Kelp was the least literate of the group, and Dreadnought had spoken in English.

"What mean 'ensign,' mighty leader?"

The other Komeopians clicked their teeth in amusement.

"Silence," Dreadnought roared. "This is a learning moment for Kelp. I have had many learning moments such as this with Professor. In those scenarios, I was as ignorant as our Kelp."

Kelp bowed nervously in thanks to Dreadnought.

"Kelp," Dreadnought said, standing with poise as he puffed out his chest. "Think of your own role here in our shiver." Dreadnought's jowls flexed performatively.

Kelp nodded eagerly, breathing through his open mouth.

"Who does Boatswain peck at?"

"Several others, several others," Kelp squeaked.

"Yes… and what about Bowsprit?"

"Some others. But never Boatswain."

"Good," Dreadnought cooed. "And what about Gunwale? Who does Gunwale peck at daily?"

"Kelp…" the scrawny Komeopian shushed himself in a panic, as if admitting it was a cultural taboo. Then, he added excitedly, "And Rudder! Gunwale pecks at Rudder."

"Yes," Dreadnought nodded. "And what about Rudder? Who does Rudder peck at?"

"Kelp," Kelp whispered again, averting his gaze away from his peers.

"Does Rudder peck at anyone else?"

Kelp shook his head. He shrank into himself, his shoulders and spikes drooping. "Only Kelp."

"And what about you," Dreadnought grumbled with encouragement. "Who do you peck at, Kelp?"

"Food," Kelp said. "Kelp pretend-es."

"But Kelp does not peck at any of his own kind,

is that right?" Dreadnought's gullet puffed up as he taunted Kelp with his condescending, maternal tone.

Kelp was not a child. He was a runt, but he seemed grown.

"Kelp no peck. No."

"That's right," Dreadnought's deep voice rolled as he mocked poor Kelp. "You are a grunt, Kelp! The runt of the shiver. You only have two jobs: follow orders and *survive*."

"Yes, Lord."

"That is what this ensign was, Kelp. Like you, his job was to take orders…" Dreadnought trailed off, lifting the ensign's corpse by the head, his plump, webbed fingers firmly gripping it. The deceased Terran's body lurched slightly as it dangled. It was awkwardly stiff with rigor mortis already. "…and to survive," Dreadnought said.

Kelp quivered but said nothing.

"Do you see how badly he has failed?" Dreadnought made a sweeping gesture, dropping the corpse. "He is your egg sack, and he's dead as a doornail."

Pappy popped up next to me again. "He's fond of Dickens, too" he said proudly.

Kelp dropped to his knees. He seemed to be gagging on air.

"What in the Rings," I muttered to myself.

Pappy was next to me. "This is how the Komeopians weep. They do not have tear glands, but rather, when they experience grief or sadness, they kick up all this extra mucus in their olfactory, and they gag on it." I still wish I didn't know that. I decided not to question such things out loud anymore.

"I don't know how you do it, Kelp," Dreadnought said with a poetic sigh. His voice rumbled in their corner of the room. "You scurry back and forth for us, always at the tail of the shiver. The same busy routine every day, and barely anything to distinguish between those days. Do you stop to question it, or are you too busy *surviving?* Is your life defined by moments like this, I wonder? When those you swim behind stop to look back and acknowledge you?"

The little Kelp hesitated. "Kelp not thinks these," he finally said, blinking lazily, one eye at a time.

"What *does* Kelp think of," Dreadnought asked. His mood was stubbornly calm and musing; Almost melodramatic, like the performance of *Hamlet* I wrote of in last issue's review of the 'Sound and Fury' cruise package aboard the *Starship Renaissance*. In only a short time, I found this Komeopian's mood shifts unsettling. As though he could hear my thoughts, Dreadnought glanced up at the room around him. All his... subjects – for truly they humored him and genuflected to his crude behavior like some spoiled monarch – stared with bated breath.

"Who told the lot of you to stop working," Dreadnought barked. "You all should have our corpse by now!"

They scurried about, hiding behind each other and ducking around corners to avoid Dreadnought's ire.

Kelp waited, his knobby joints quivering. He watched Dreadnought, desperate for a social cue so he knew what to do. Bobbing around, he kept ducking his head even lower, no doubt as a sign of submission to those around him.

After a moment of this uncertainty, Dreadnought weighed in. "Back to work, Kelp. My pondering is over." The bass of Dreadnought's voice alone seemed like a threat. Kelp squealed, rushing away to a corpse in the corner behind me. Dreadnought crossed his arms, surveying his shiver like a corporate manager.

Before long, the dark green Komeopian, Gunwale, pinpointed a sergeant's corpse among their carnage. I watched as he bowed to his leader, offering the head up as though it were on a platter. His shocking blue eyes flashed in the dark room, glowing with the indigo running lights around us.

Dreadnought wasted no time in swiping the disembodied head for himself. The lifeless Terran skull thunked against the security panel, held there by Dreadnought's overwhelmingly large, webbed hand.

The retinal scanner flashed red, and the security panel bleated in confirmation. With a groan, the heavy security doors slid open, revealing the hallway I'd been down for my visit with the captain.

It was on to the Command Bridge.

12. COMMAND BRIDGE

The Komeopians shuffled forth, wielding clear riot shields retrieved from a vault in the security barracks. A few of them had donned helmets, and many of them traded their makeshift weapons for the standard issue short swords they found hanging on the walls.

As his rampart of mutinous fish marched forward, forming a line of protection with their shields, Dreadnought stopped in the doorway and reached for something mounted over the blast doors.

With a vicious growl, his arm lurched away from the wall. He came down with a Cliptorgian broadsword; a hefty, 't' shaped sword with a blade of zevver, the glittering purple alloy of my homeworld.

The severe blade was fitted with three amber gems near the hilt. They were not of a stone I recognized. As they marched forward, the lights flickered. An alarm thonked eagerly, and a computerized voice echoed to us from the bridge. "Warning: mechanical failure in power stack three. Rerouting the command bridge to auxiliary power."

Just then, something in the ceiling crackled and popped. The overhead running lights cut out, and we were doused in a calming ultraviolet glow. Auxiliary floodlights flickered at the other end of the hallway as we marched, flashing like vengeful summer lightning. I heard frantic shouts from the Command Bridge ahead. The doors lurched wide open, no doubt coaxed by the power drain.

On the bridge, just beyond those doors, the captain and his deck crew scrambled. They were hemmed in unless they risked breaching the foredeck blast doors. I doubted they would. Some starliner companies even had policies forbidding it. Those mechanisms were meant for emergency evacuations only.

Two security officers poked their heads around the corner of the open doors ahead of us. They were outfitted like those who lay dead in the barracks behind us. The officer on the right shouted something unintelligible at us. As he did, I noticed the other one produce a black orb and pull a pin from it. Then, he rolled the orb at us. It was hissing as it bounced.

"Varaan kuhl," I cussed under my breath. Then, I ducked, turning around so my back was to the impending blast. In a moment of reflex, I squared my shoulders and held Dreadnought back, too.

Bang!

A bright burst of hot, white light flashed before us, washing out the ultraviolet auxiliary lights. Green and bruise-colored splotches danced across my field of vision. I clenched my eyes shut, gasping in surprise at the pain. My ears rang in the concussive aftermath, and for a moment, the chaos around me was muted: muffled as though I were underwater.

The line of Komeopians ahead of us scattered, dropping their formation, shields clattering to the floor. As their defensive form collapsed, the mutineers to either side rushed forward into the Command Bridge, whooping and roaring and shrieking in rage.

Two of Dreadnaught's shiver collapsed in shock. One I recognized as Bowsprit and another I had not managed to acquaint myself with. Though the orb seemed only to be a flash grenade, its concussive blast completely disoriented them. Bowsprit clenched his eyes, while the other target convulsed on the floor.

It didn't matter.

Both the security officers in the doorway were felled by the surge of Komeopian fury the blast instigated. My heart sank as I accounted for those two dead security officers. Finding them told me there were now only three other security officers onboard to account for. I'd witnessed the deaths of fifteen, and *Ichthus* was not large enough to alter spacefaring protocols. In truth, eighteen security officers together may not have stood a better chance, I admitted. That thought made the floor spin out from under me, and I extended my arms in a moment of dizziness. In response, Dreadnought reached down to steady me.

"Are you injured," he asked. His voice cracked with genuine concern. Was he growing fond of me?

I blinked hard, still shaking the bruised splotches from my vision. "I'll be fine," I said. "I'm sure that was terrible for my eyes, but what's done is done." I blinked and looked up at him. "Are you good," I asked in return.

"I am unscathed, and you have gained my favor." He nodded like some valiant knight off to defend my honor. Then, he hefted the Cliptorgian broadsword and churned angrily onto the bridge. I smiled at his classical melodrama, rolling my eyes ever so slightly. There was something about *that* side of Dreadnought I couldn't help but be amused by.

He stopped in the center of the room, facing the captain, who was trying not to appear as though he was hiding behind the ship's wheel. His remaining two protectorates flanked him on either side of the helm controls. From their dark green uniforms, I suspected they were armed deck officers and not specialized security.

"Cowards!" Dreadnought's voice rumbled around the room. "Face me valiantly or die *slowly!*"

The captain's guards were Cliptorgian women: Till[16], more specifically. One was armed with an axe

---

[16] A sect of Cliptorgians who continue ancient education and fighting techniques of their planet's past. They are often hired as mercenaries and mediators in socio-political situations throughout

and the other with her own Cliptorgian broadsword. The captain clamored behind the Till with the axe, pulling her in front of him as he went.

Dreadnought rushed them both, reaching out with his left flipper to hold the Till's axe down. His right arm hefted his sword, and in one vicious swipe, he lobbed the Till's head off.

The captain yelped. His other Till protector hefted her broadsword, the blade held defiantly in Dreadnought's direction. She struck low on Dreadnought's sword, near the hilt, and, in reflex, he flung her back hard. The power behind just one of his arms was so immense, the Till clattered against the wall behind her, slamming her head. I saw Dreadnought wind up with his sword, bringing both hands to bear on its leathern hilt. I'd seen a similar image once aboard the *ISF Good Sport*, a military cruise in collaboration with several major sports leagues, most of them Terran. Dreadnought wound up, his form striking the same aggressive pose as a hefty baseball batter. But Dreadnought wasn't aiming at a ball.

---

the universe because of their training, which emphasizes equal reverence of intellectual and martial prowess. The Till have defined themselves as a unique subculture of Cliptorgian society, but the group's ideals stem from the practices of one individual: Elvira Till. Considered the founder of Till practices, Elvira struck out to perfect herself physically and mentally upon deciding not to bear children. Her surname Till distinguishes her lineage as one of the seven 'Family Clans of Cliptorgia.' The Clans are so ancient, the constellations of Cliptorgia tell tales of their exploits. Elvira is considered 'The Mother of Modern Reason.'

He leered as he towered over the disoriented Till officer. She ducked under his blade, and Dreadnought's sword clanged off the wall. The Till swung her blade as she ducked under the force of Dreadnought's clattering blow. He torqued brutishly, swinging his weapon wildly at his target.

The Till woman's sword struck Dreadnought's chainmail, but the tip of the blade nicked into his underarm. He howled in painful agitation and jerked his elbow back hard.

It was only then that I noted the Komeopian's quill-like spines. They ran in a spiked pattern along the outer forearm like nature's own gauntlets. Those spiked quills jerked down on the Till's head, at the base of her skull, as she was ducking past.

I saw the whites of her eyes as they went wide with shock. She uttered only half a groan as I heard the sickening plunk of punctured flesh.

The Till woman collapsed face-first on the helm, clearly defeated. Regardless, Dreadnought seemed in a blood rage. His pupils were dilated, wide and lifeless and black. He twirled around, hoisting his sword over his head. He swung hard at the Till officer's body, hacking away... defacing her.

For the sake of the Till clan's culture, I must stress that the officer fought valiantly. There was no way for me to learn her surname, so her warrior's memory may never truly be honored. Though her end was undignified, her fighting spirit was not...

"Hey, hey, hey, hey, hey," Pappy chanted, holding

out a hand to try and subdue his raging pupil.

Dreadnaught paused, his jagged teeth working in his slack jaw. He breathed heavily, moisture and mucous gurgling under his forked tongue, then raised his sword over his lifeless victim again. As I opened my mouth to protest, I was blindsided by a flash of bruising pain that hit me from behind and I collapsed to the floor.

The world around me grew black, shrouded in a hazy fog that threatened to whisk me away. Another thud of pain pulled me, gasping, back to consciousness. As the world came into focus, I distinguished the captain's voice babbling above me.

"Stupid bitch! Stupid, self-righteous Cliptorgian bitch!" From my quick assessment, he'd tackled me to the floor, and now sat atop my legs, swinging wildly with closed fists. I shielded the front of myself with my forearms and kicked hard until I knocked his barrel-shaped belly off kilter. At the same time, Pappy moved to intervene. He hefted a riot shield, swinging the edge of it at the captain's belly. As it bashed into the old brute, he crumpled into a wheezing ball.

Dreadnought roared over to us, pushing both Pappy and me away from the captain. The Komeopian raised his sword at Englehorn.

"Wait," I hesitated aloud.

Dreadnought had his back to us. He did not turn, just stared down at the wheezing captain. His webbed fingers worked their grip on his sword's hilt. "He is my captain, therefore my captor. He is my captor;

126

therefore, he is my prey."

"Yes," I stammered, "yes, of course. But he can give you control of this ship… if you force him to."

Dreadnought was silent.

The captain panted still, glaring at me from behind the glint of the big Komeopian's blade. "Treacherous bitch!"

Without warning, Dreadnought flinched, his whole left arm striking down at the captain's face.

The captain cried out, collapsing to the floor. He spat blood from a bleeding cheek.

"You are the bitch," Dreadnought spat at Englehorn. The Komeopian then turned to me. "How does he give me control? I want to kill this swine and wear his crown."

"Autopilot," I said, taking a moment to shoot the captain a defiant look. "They call it Auto. It's activated via voice command." I was done considering sides. After the Komeopian show of force, I believed my best bet for survival lay in the hands of Dreadnought's people. Captain Englehorn would win no battles today. I might as well expedite this violent uprising and further earn Dreadnought's trust in the process.

"So, if I kill him now, we must control the ship ourselves?"

"Yes. And I'm sure you're prepared to do that. But maintaining control would be so much easier with all the ship's automated functions at your fingertips."

Pappy stepped forward as I said this. "I am prepared," the old man said. "I've stood at the helm of more than a few ships in my day."

"But only he can relinquish voice command to someone else. Dreadnought, if you are to command the *Ichthus*, to 'wear the crown,' as you say, you should strategically position yourself with as much power as possible. Give yourself a captain's full privilege; use the vessel's automated systems to your advantage and secure your spot at the head of your shiver." I simply had no idea where this maniacal side of me had come from, but I was not about to faulter.

Pappy's eyes flickered nervously at me now. Something about them warned me off the subject, like an angry parent shooting daggers at an unruly child. Did Pappy distrust Dreadnought on some level? If so, it was too late for me to withhold.

Dreadnought raised the point of his blade to the captain's throat. "Do what she says."

"Not unless you agree to let me live."

Dreadnought laughed defiantly. "After all your beatings? After the electric water? And the toxic engine fluids that still stain my gills with their chlorinated stench? No, sir… no!" He barked the last 'no' with such force, it reverberated around the room in a low rumble. "The only salvation you may seek is a merciful death. But you will die. Either way, I have claimed Angwari on your soul. Your life is mine to take!"

"Now, we've been through this," Pappy piped up. "That is not for anyone to say." He waited as Dreadnought stared blankly at him. Finally, he added, "You can take the ship, yes, but you can*not* keep up with these superstitions. Komeopian Law does not exist here!"

"Komeopian law exists wherever there are Komeopians! If you dislike it, you should take it up with those who drugged us in the night and dragged us here in *coffins!* No, Professor. I shall lead my people the way I see fit. Our own laws shall govern the *Starship Ichthus*, not yours." He snatched up the enfeebled captain with one great, hulking arm. "Show me Autopilot now, and you may yet die quickly."

Tears gathered in the captain's eyes, but I could not feel pity for him. "This is your doing, Artemus," he hissed at Pappy. "My blood is on *your* hands, sailor!" He wept, simpering as Dreadnought heaved with rage.

"And the blood of how many did my shiver lose under the crack of your cruel whip?" Dreadnought howled his accusation like a funeral dirge. "Did you count them, eh? Do you know their numbers? Or their worth among our elders for the generational knowledge they retained?"

"We didn't know you could speak," the captain pleaded. "They didn't tell us any of that. We didn't know you could think… or *feel*."

"Were our cries not enough? The howling fits when we mourned our countless dead?"

Captain Englehorn could only sob. "I'm… sorry. I'm sorry. Please?" He grabbed at Dreadnought's grip on his shirt collar, but the Komeopian stood firm, shaking the sniveling man.

"Autopilot. Now!"

The captain's face turned red, and his tears melted away in an impulse of indignant anger. "Kill me," he spat, his fear morphing into belligerence before us all. "But if I die, I'm taking Autopilot with me, you fish-breathed fuck-face!" The captain hollered his insult.

Dreadnought roared. It was a primal, howling sound that shattered any other noise around us.

To his credit, old Englehorn held his ground, his feet firmly planted to the bridge. Saliva spattered his beard, but he lifted his head. His legs, however, were shaking so hard they had his pants snapping like sails against a mighty wind. The only relief he found was in the puddle of urine that formed slowly at his heel after seeping through his crisp, white pant leg.

Seeing this, Dreadnought blinked. He reached down and pushed the old man over, his boots screeching on the wet black floor of the Command Bridge. Next, Dreadnought pounced, his knees landing on the captain's left leg. I cringed, hearing the pop of a dislocated joint, and swallowed the lump in my throat before it could make me physically sick.

The captain screamed.

"Mizzenmast?" Dreadnought belched. "Bring me a gut-skipper."

A hefty Komeopian with puckered scars on his face lurched forward from guarding the open doorway behind us. He held out an indigo jelly sack no larger than a strawberry. I spied spindly black legs, like those of a small crustacean, skittering about and poking the jelly membrane from the inside.

Dreadnought took the jelly sack, grabbed the captain's throat with his free hand, and squeezed until the tortured man opened his mouth. Englehorn gagged in shock, and Dreadnought stuffed the indigo pouch down the captain's gullet. The Komeopian held his hand over Captain Englehorn's mouth as the old man squirmed. After a few seconds, though, the captain's white beard was flooded with a drizzle of thick purple bile. The inky goo gushed out between Dreadnought's fingers, and he grinned maliciously. "Just swallow, and I'll let you breathe again," he cooed into the captain's ear.

The captain was reduced to weeping once more. The bridge was silent as the grave while we waited to see Englehorn's throat muscles contract. Those few moments took a lifetime. Did he not want his discomfort to end?

Finally, the captain gulped.

Dreadnought let him go, cackling as he did. "You air-suckers, you're all so feeble! Only one way to breathe in!" The room of Komeopians erupted in hateful cackles, and more of their damned teeth clattering. That wet, harsh clicking noise chilled my very bones.

"Uuuggghh," the captain moaned, staggering backwards and groping at air to steady himself. "What was that? What did you do to me?"

"I have given you your slow death, Captain." Dreadnought sat himself in the captain's chair, his head held high as he looked down at Englehorn, who groveled on the floor before him. Dreadnought chuckled, leering at the captain. "I hope you had a big dinner."

"What did I swallow, damn you? What's inside me?"

"The Melcorian gut-skipper is a strange creature. You see, on our home world, they live in sulfur fields and around geysers along the ocean floor. Their exoskeleton is resistant to highly acidic environments, so they can go where other bottom feeders can't. And they scavenge meat and microorganisms in those hostile places." Dreadnought smiled wickedly, leaning in. The captain shrunk away from the big brute. "There's another place I've found they can live... in the bellies of our foes! That gut-skipper will make merry for a few hours, eating away at what's left in your stomach. But they feed nonstop. And eventually, your belly will be empty, except for all that fleshy stomach lining."

The captain quivered. "It's going to eat its way out of my belly," he nodded, his voice trembling.

Dreadnought pursed his lips. "No, not necessarily. The gut-skipper is unpredictable. Sometimes they'll nibble out your naval, yes. But other times, they'll scratch and claw at your esophagus. Why, sometimes they follow the food supply through your intestinal tract. I've even seen a few gnaw their way out of an anus!" His smile curled with sickening satisfaction.

As if on cue, the captain's belly grumbled. "What? I—" Englehorn did not finish his thought but instead tore wildly at his shirt. In his panic, he stripped away his overcoat, then all but ripped off his tie and button-down shirt. He clawed at the tuft of white hair that evenly powdered his rounded torso. "Get it out! Get it out," he begged us all, his voice cracking as he broke into hysterics.

"No," Dreadnought bellowed, pulling a vial of red liquid from a pouch on his belt. "If you give me access to Autopilot, I will administer the antidote. But if you don't… well, then you *will* die, Captain Englehorn. We will watch with joy as our pet devours you from the inside out."

The captain fell to his knees before Dreadnought like a priest before a dais. "Okay. Okay, I'll help. Just don't let me die this way…. Please. Not this way!"

"Good," Dreadnought nodded. "You see, I get what I want," he bragged, turning in his chair to glare pointedly at Pappy. "The tides favor my claim of Angwari, Professor. You are wrong about my Gods."

Pappy glowered in the shadows.

"Proceed, Captain," Dreadnought commanded curtly. "I grow weary of your tears."

"Auto," the captain said, struggling to stop his voice from quaking with fear. He pressed that center button on the helm's num-pad. and the console raised, revealing the cube that was Autopilot the Android.

"Activate Starship *Ichthus* Autopilot. Voice ID pattern: Captain Englehorn."

The console beeped with approval, and the little skeletal android Auto unfolded before us. Its amber eyes glowed in the relatively dark Command Bridge. The Komeopians clicked their teeth with awe as the little android saluted the captain.

"The captain appears distressed," Auto's nasally, robotic voice reported. "I will sound the alarm."

"No, no," the captain corrected. "Auto, there was… an accident. But! I've been saved. Therefore, I must relinquish command to…" he trailed off, pointing at Dreadnought with a subtle shrug.

"Dreadnought," the Komeopian growled. "You yourself named me, you wretch! Are we *that* forgettable? Are we *that* faceless?"

Auto's copper metal head shook, his neck joints whirring softly. "Is the captain certain this is a sound command decision?"

Dreadnought scoffed. "Even your synthetics are xenophobes," he spat. "A plague of algae on all your hides."

"Auto is merely following protocol," the captain said somewhat wearily. "He is programmed to ensure my safety. If he suspects that I am injured, as I have indeed been, then his protocol is to express concern." The captain turned back to the copper android skeleton. "Auto, there is nothing you need to worry about." I saw the captain subconsciously grab at his bare belly.

He wasn't lying, I thought, considering that Auto was not a MedBot.

"I am hereby relinquishing command to Dreadnought. Do as he says, so long as it doesn't interfere with your protocol overrides."

"Affirmative. Autopilot logs the change in command at oh-two-hundred hours. Voice recognition Code Bravo. Dreadnought, please state your name and rank so that I may adjust my voice match protocol."

The Komeopian bristled with pride, standing up tall. "Captain Dreadnought," he stated boisterously.

Auto's belly bleeped in denial. The android's eyes blinked red three times at us before returning to their calm, amber glow. "Error: please indicate a surname."

Dreadnought's eyes were panic-stricken. "Dread-*nought*. Nought. And Dread."

"Thank you, Captain Knot-head," the android said as its computing systems chirped with acceptance.

Pappy and the captain both stifled a laugh. Dreadnought snarled. "Call me Captain Dreadnought, damn you!"

"I understand, Captain Dreadnought Damn-you."

"Aaahhh!" The beastly alien exploded, raising a fist at Auto. Hesitation overtook Dreadnought in mere milliseconds before he redirected his blow at the captain's chair, denting its smooth metal side. "Do not mock me," the angry tyrant yelled. "Not any of you!" He turned back to the android. "Disable the ship's Automa… Automat…" He frowned, pulling a string of seashells from a back pocket. I could see several notes scratched into their scooped bellies. As Dreadnought peered at each shell, I realized he was reading them. He did so slowly, tasting each word as he did. "Here! Disable the Automatic Protocol

Response Systems for the engine coolant valves. Increase pressure of storage valves ten through forty."

"Affirmative, Captain Damn-you," Auto said with a salute. The skeletal copper android stepped in front of the helm and started rapidly punching buttons.

Dreadnought scowled but kept his temper. He waited a moment, observing Auto blissfully. I could tell he savored the control. Then, a new thought occurred to him, relaxing his face into a satisfied smile. He grabbed the bulky Com from Pappy's toolbelt. "Boatswain," he barked.

The Com speaker buzzed, then: "Yes, mighty one?"

"Team Fleg may start the flood," Dreadnought instructed. Behind him, Kelp giggled, chattering his spindly teeth.

"What the hell are you planning," Englehorn demanded.

"These conditions," Dreadnought said, sweeping his arm through the cool, synthetic air around him, "they are not suitable for my crew. We require more water…"

He smiled his wicked smile at us. "This might be a good time to grow some gills, *air-suckers*."

13. THANKLESS CHILD

"What are you playing at, you brute," Captain Englehorn challenged.

"Article IV of the Interstellar Captain's Oath," Dreadnought gloated. "'In a survival situation, it is the captain's duty to maintain suitable living conditions for his crew.'"

Captain Englehorn stared incredulously at him. Dreadnought merely blinked with expectation. When Englehorn showed no understanding, Dreadnought shot me a knowing glance and rolled his eyes. Then, he placed a thick, webbed hand on Autopilot's shoulder. "Auto," he spat, "increase water valve pressure by fifty percent."

"Aye, aye, sir," Auto said innocently with a salute.

"What's in your head," Englehorn snapped.

"Wait and see, old man. Wait and see." Dreadnought leaned back, crossing his arms.

Just then, Auto swiveled over to Dreadnought and saluted him. The android's voice box chimed, "Your maintenance requests have been executed, Captain Damn-you."

Dreadnought cringed; Auto continued to mislabel him 'Captain Damn-you.' I found it fitting enough… as if the ship's inner voice was subconsciously cursing Dreadnought for the destruction he was exacting on it.

Dreadnought tapped the communications console. "Boatswain, report back."

The Com speaker hissed, then: "Aye, sir. All tanks are reading at maximum pressure."

"Break the seals," Dreadnought commanded.

"What," Englehorn wailed.

In response, Dreadnought swung an open hand that cracked across the captain's cheek.

I yelped in shock as the old Terran crumpled to the floor. He glared at Dreadnought, his face turning bright red.

"Keep your objections out of my orders," Dreadnought growled.

"Give me my antidote," the captain pleaded, reaching a frail hand up in surrender.

Towering over old Englehorn, Dreadnought regarded his surrender, then paused. He turned to the android. "Auto," he asked, cooing the robot's name.

"Yes, Captain Damn-you?"

Dreadnought's brow furrowed again with agitation. "Under what circumstances would you stop taking orders from me?"

"Why, if Captain Englehorn's voice match ordered an override of his previous command."

"And if that voice command never comes?"

"I continue to follow your orders, Captain."

"Under *any* circumstances?"

"Aye, sir. That is protocol. Under any and all circumstances."

Dreadnought sucked a deep breath in through the tiny air holes on his big face where a nose might have been. I saw his gills flex at the base of his head, along his jaw line. In that moment, I seemed to recall learning that gills were a sensitive spot-on larger water breathing animals. This was true of Terran sharks as well as the grots[17] of Cliptorgian seas. If I felt physically threatened, perhaps I'd chance testing the theory on my Komeopian captors.

Dreadnought was nodding dramatically and pointing to a star chart. "Auto, you have the bridge. Maintain course until we're a full day's journey from the Great Barrier[18]. Then, kill the engines and contact me via my personal Com." Dreadnought waved his Com over the helm, which chimed pleasantly and glowed green for a moment.

"Affirmative," Auto said, gripping the helm and

---

[17] A predatory, eel-like creature native to the major oceans of Cliptorgia. They grow roughly three meters long from snout to tail and are often compared in shape to 'an uncurled seahorse.'

[18] Comprised of billions of force field emitters networked around the star systems containing Cliptorgia and Earth, the Great Barrier isolates the ISF and its trade routes from the rest of the universe.

turning away.

Dreadnought turned back to the captain, who was still on the floor. "Old man," he growled, pulling Englehorn up by his shirt collar. The captain straightened up. He had to lean back to lock eyes with the Komeopian leader. Dreadnought merely held out the red vial. "Come with us. Retrieve what you have earned." With that, Dreadnought left the bridge, stepping out into the hallway. Once there, he nodded for his shiver to huddle up. Dreadnought's people followed him closely. They leaned in, forcing me into the middle of their circle. The stench of brine and barnacles exposed to air billowed around us in a stifling bog.

In the huddle, I lost sight of Pappy. To my surprise, Dreadnought handed the captain his red vial of gut-skipper antidote and released his grip on the man's shirt.

Englehorn scrambled forward, staggering for balance once he was free of all resistance. "Oh," he wept, "oh, thank you." He gulped down the vial just a few meters away.

In hushed tones, Dreadnought confided in his shiver. "You have all heard it with me; I have full control of the ship," Dreadnought said. "I am its true captain. The old man is of no further use to us. I claim Angwari on his soul."

"I bear witness," Gunwale, the dark green Komeopian said, nodding.

"Kelp also," Kelp offered.

"I do also," the one called Spar confided.

Dreadnought gave a quick, sharp nod. "The time has come." The kingly fish grumbled with satisfaction.

"Ack-" Captain Englehorn cried out. His outburst was punctuated by the unmistakable *shink* of a blade shearing through meat and bone. Before any of us could blink, Englehorn's head was lobbed clean off. The man's body slumped to the floor, and his head and hat went rolling away behind a column of damned decorative pipes.

As the captain's decapitated body dropped, Pappy's panting frame stood over it. He was unable to maintain the Cliptorgian Broadsword, which he must have retrieved from the downed Till on the bridge. He let the tip sag to the floor, then adjusted so he was holding the hilt out in front of him with the blade pointed down. He looked like a knight in a guard stance.

The Komeopians gathered around, tittering quietly for a moment before their banter reached crescendo, and they all broke into a chorus of cheers.

Dreadnought gritted his needle teeth. "No," he bellowed, bounding forward. He landed on Englehorn's headless corpse, pushing Pappy back as he did. The old sailor staggered to the floor, the broadsword clattering. Kelp rushed to his side.

"Pappy, no," I cried out. I couldn't help myself. "Why would you do that?"

Pappy glared at me, then shifted his red-hot gaze on his pupil… his intellectual progeny. "There is no antidote," he hissed. "You gave him poison, didn't you, Dread?"

Dreadnought growled, the immense clicking in the back of his throat sent a chill down my back. Then, he snapped. Like a wild boar, he bucked and flailed and punched at Englehorn's stiff, headless corpse. As he carried on, his hammering caused gore to spurt from the neck with his most forceful blows.

I stifled my reflex to heave.

"Child," Pappy continued, shaking his head. "There is no antidote for a gut-skipper," Pappy was explaining to me, but he spoke loud enough so that his words were also for Dreadnought's benefit. "That was a poisonous brine. It'll kill the gut-skipper, sure enough," Pappy paused and took a deep breath. His voice rattled in his chest a bit. "But it would've killed the captain slowly while lulling him into psychedelic hallucinations… it would have played into every paranoia he's ever had and broken his mind. I'n't that right, Dreadnought?"

The Komeopian leader roared, hammering his massive fists on Englehorn's chest like a toddler on a drum kit. Something in the cadaver's chest cracked violently.

"Answer me!" Pappy was glaring at his pupil again. Dreadnought finally stopped, locked eyes with Pappy, and intentionally dug his claws into Englehorn's bleeding chest. Next, Dreadnought looked around to his shiver and said proudly, "Though those that are betrayed do feel the treason sharply, yet the traitor stands in worse case of woe."

Pappy gathered his lips and jutted out his chin. "How sharper than a serpent's tooth it is to have a thankless child." I heard the edge of scorn in his voice.

"I claimed Angwari on his soul," Dreadnought accused. "It was my right to torment him!" Once again, he turned to his shiver. "Tell him!"

"Angwari was claimed," big Gunwale grumbled first.

"It is truth," Spar nodded vigorously.

"It's impolite to mutilate the dead," Pappy barked. "And it brings terrible luck out among the stars."

Dreadnought threw up his arms and shouted. There were no words to go with his protestations. And then, he paused… and leaned into Pappy. "You have lost my trust." He said calmly and with far too much ease for someone who had just thrown a tantrum. I made a conscious effort not to take a step back.

"Then that makes us even." Pappy didn't miss a beat. "Either way, the captain is dead, like you wanted. You got to scare the piss out of him – literally – and you had the satisfaction of making him yield full control of his ship to you. Like you wanted. He suffered. You made him suffer. Like you wanted. You tortured his mind from the moment you ran through that doorway. Isn't that enough?"

Dreadnought huffed air through his gills in frustration. "No."

"I warned you this couldn't be a mutiny fueled by revenge. No man deserves–"

143

"Artemis!" Dreadnought belched Pappy's name like an agitated mother at the end of her rope. "Do not dare finish that thought. You witnessed the captain's menace firsthand! Is that not why you chose to mentor me?"

"Yes, but—"

"Did you not tell me yourself that you despised his lack of *humanity* for other creatures?"

"I did." Pappy's shoulders sagged.

"Then you admit we deserved Angwari. An eye for an eye."

I didn't hear what Pappy muttered in reply, but I did see Dreadnought shake his head as he plucked Captain Englehorn's dark green hat up off the floor.

Dreadnought paused, digging around in a corner of the hallway where several Terran corpses were strewn about. He produced Englehorn's head. Blood trickled from the base of its neck, and Pappy jumped back to avoid being splattered with it.

"Somehow," the big brute sighed, gazing into the captain's lifeless face, "I believe you're right. There is no satisfaction in exacting a torturous revenge." He tossed the head aside. "From now on, my foes will face a quick death." As he smiled to himself, alarms rang out around the Command Bridge. My throat twisted in a knot as the ship's shrill sirens shattered the philosophical tension.

Auto zipped over to the door, his amber eyes searching until they found Dreadnought in the hallway. "Captain Damn-you, sensors indicate a drop in emergency coolant levels for Stack Three and Stack Four."

Dreadnought smiled. "Disregard that. Seal off the bridge and remain at the helm."

"Aye, sir." If an android could second guess orders, Auto proved it to me in that moment.

The thick metal doors of the Command Bridge groaned as they eased out of the wall. They seemed reluctant to close, and I stepped forward so I could better make out the readouts on the port wall, where two dozen security monitors cycled through camera feeds from various locations aboard the *Ichthus*.

The ship's alarms rang out over every security feed. "Warning: flooding detected," the loudspeakers screamed at us. Dreadnought shook his head, shielding his ears with his flippered hands. Seizing the opportunity, Pappy turned to me, leaning close to my ear. His voice was loud, clear, and calm in my head over the chaos rattling around us. "You should escape when the flood comes."

He gave me no opportunity to react. Instead, he turned to Dreadnought, who was covering his ears and howling.

"You want the noise to stop," Pappy said to the childish Komeopian.

"Aye," Dreadnought belched. "Mightily."

"Ask the robot," Pappy instructed, nodding to Auto.

Dreadnought puffed out his chest and hollered to Auto, who was continually rushing from station to station checking on ship's systems. "Autopilot," Dreadnought commanded, "Auto," Dreadnought shouted. "Disable all safety alarms ship wide." He pointed his left index finger – the only one he had left thanks to me – at Auto like a determined king.

"Right away, sir," Autopilot said, saluting the towering fish. His slight, skeletal body zipped over to the security console and, in a flurry of his copper fingers, disabled the terrible noises. The hefty doors to the Command Bridge finally lurched shut, hissing as they sealed us off.

The entire hallway fell silent as the grave. I daresay all we could hear after that was the creaking, groaning echoes of a starship that I did not realize yet was soaking through to the bone. In that silence, the solitary security feed in our corner of the hallway switched to a grand room with dark crimson velvet and gold accents. It was clearly the luxurious casino, for I could see the Blackjack tables from one of the cycling camera angles. It was labeled 'Aft Deck A,' which meant it was somewhere behind us on the same level.

At first, I wasn't sure what I was seeing; the walls of the casino seemed to be leaking water. In some spots, fonts of it poured slowly from seams along the ceiling. The liquid was toxically green, and based on Dreadnought's claims, I suspected it was saturated with an unimaginable number of chemicals. Passengers were panicking all through the still-busy venue. At least a dozen passengers lingered by the cashier's cage, no doubt hesitant to leave without cashing out.

A fresh feed from the starboard side showed the leaking cracks dancing across the decorative stained-glass fixture above them all. The seams gave; water and glass doused the gamblers and night owls who were retreating below.

Involuntarily, I gasped.

Dreadnought turned to me, noting the security feeds I was observing. He chuckled with satisfaction, a deep, vibrating chortle that resonated through my chest.

"Oh, look," he mused, pointing to one feed where several cabin doors slid open all at once, no doubt stirred by the roaring torrent of water rushing down the hall. In seconds, they were swept away in the angry white foam. A secondary gush of water swept around the far end of the tunnel. It crashed into the security camera, and the feed malfunctioned in a maelstrom of bubbles.

14. THE FLOOD

My heart fluttered in my chest. I stifled a cry of shock; the bastards were drowning everyone! Innocent passengers were swallowed up in camera angle after camera angle as that surging, toxic water overtook the upper decks.

Pappy turned away. Slyly, he produced a large silver flask from his coat pocket. How many times had I missed him sneak a swig throughout this damned overthrow? Not that I was surprised. It made sense for the old man who was drunk by noon at our first social outing.

I could see the old sailor's hands were shaking like pale, dead leaves in an autumn breeze. Although he covered his face, I spied tears dropping to the floor. Two of them pattered off the edge of his boat shoes. It was hard for me to feel bad for him.

As the feed switched again, the waterline in the

casino was rising rapidly. The water lapped at the camera until, in a cascade of churning bubbles, the device was fully submerged. Right before the feed cut out, I recognized Boatswain slicing through the water like a furious eel. He led a group of Komeopians; I assumed that was 'Team Fleg' coming to join us.

The water was near, roaring in agony the way an ocean roars when it's spoiling for a storm. Water was pooling in from cracks and seams in the walls and dribbling down from the rafters above us. I only took two steps before I froze with fear. The rampaging, aimless water came crashing out through the casino's blast doors, at the far end of the hallway. It funneled in a foaming white fury directly at our party of mutineers. The water spilled out into the hallway around us first, then its force flanked us, hammering us from the sides before washing everyone away.

Pappy jumped in front of me at the last minute as the rush of toxic green water crashed over his shoulders, the last thing he said to me was, "Save yourself!"

The water consumed us. It cascaded down from the rafters, washed us away with the blood on the floors. I was soaked through in the blink of an angry eye, my clothing pressed against me. The water's silky liquid touch left me colder than ice. Time slowed to that sickeningly patient tempo of the dead, and I have no clue how long those dark flood waters held us captive.

Sound moved slowly to me underwater. My skin burned slightly, as though I'd applied aloe to an open wound. The same sensation stung my nostrils, and a distinct chlorine tang shocked my olfactory. My head spun, and my eyes were on fire. I could not imagine filtering such foul things through my lungs or throat. Lightheadedness crept in on me. It was just like what I had experienced breathing the boggy smog down Pappy's hatch. To experience it every hour of every day, as I knew the Komeopians had, seemed more torturous than the quick deaths they'd given the ship's security team.

The Komeopians were all swimming freely as the hallway was completely submerged. They congregated around the doors to Lift 1 and Lift 2 along the interior wall. I saw the powerful frames of two larger Komeopians swim up to the elevator doors. Gunwale, the dark green Komeopian, and Boatswain, the tall, muscular one, clawed and scratched, prying the lift doors open with their mighty webbed feet. The doors shrieked as they gave way, and the water around us was siphoned into the elevator shafts. The pressure in my head grew thick and painful. My clothing was plastered to me, pressed so tightly I wanted to flail for more space.

The Komeopians succeeded, for the pressure from the water tore the maimed elevator doors away. I saw the water swirl like a great whirlpool, and it sucked Kelp away from us, as if he'd gone down a drain. My chest was tight and desperate for breath, so I kicked, rushing to follow him.

As I passed through those doors, I tumbled into the lift, snagging a gulp of air as the water sprayed out around me into the dark space of the empty elevator shaft. Then, I was forced below crashing waves again. I tumbled in wet, chaotic darkness. A webbed hand grabbed my arm and pulled me back. Gunwale held up some underwater lantern in the darkness. He was holding me back. We waited as Dreadnought swam up to the glowing console next to the doors labeled 'Deck B' overhead. The big Komeopian seemed to float through the water in slow motion.

My lungs tugged at my throat even though they'd been momentarily relieved. They begged me to suck in air and whatever else was around me. I held fast, but that made my headache throb worse between my temples.

Dreadnought waved his right flipper in front of the console. The readout changed from the red message 'Sealed for Emergency' to the yellow warning 'Emergency Manual Override.' The lift doors cracked open, and the water around us in the shaft-turned-pipe spilled forth. I flopped out onto the familiar tiled floors of Deck B.

I heaved for air. My throat burned with the subtle splash of liquid I'd sucked in. Was Pappy still with us? How long could he hold his breath? I wasn't sure if he was still being dragged along, or if he'd managed at all. My mind raced on.

The trickling water gushed to the floor, pooling there as the patterned tiles came alive beneath me in the rippling liquid. My lungs shuddered for their vital resource. The geometric black and white patterns waggled underwater around me like a curious school of swimming Rorschach tests.

As I knelt there, the water thundered into the hallway around me like a burst water main. Occasionally, the rush would give birth to a Komeopian soldier. I had lost count of them all when Team Fleg joined the picture. They outnumbered me greatly, which was all that mattered.

Somewhere in the back of my mind, a string quartet was playing merrily. I heard an air-breather's lungs cough behind me, near the surging elevator waterfall. It was Pappy. I turned to him as soon as my head stopped spinning.

Pappy only frowned, his lungs rattling with liquid. He coughed, the sound rattling through his frail, wet frame. He knelt there in the pool of water, his body a fit of tremors, and the Komeopians merely stared.

"Help him," I begged.

The Komeopians shushed me in unison, united in their vocalization. They were down in the murky knee-deep waters. They allowed their heads to lurk just above the rising waterline like crocodiles. It was too dark under the auxiliary blue lights to see their bodies crouched and straining to keep them submerged in the shallow waters, but I imagined it when I realized it was hard to tell what they were. Seeing only their crown-like spiking heads atop the water was like finding sinister potted cacti bobbing about in a flood.

I silenced my gasping for air, but there was really no need. The water was seeping through cracks in the ceiling above us, and it thundered around us like some tropical waterfall crashing into a cavernous pool. Pappy coughed again, reaching for me. His breath carried the musty sting of liquor and the dry stench of moth balls. I tried not to notice, but when I did, my stomach was instead churned by the bog of sea stench in the raging waters rising around us.

The Komeopians turned from us, the emergency blue running lights glinting in their eyes like icicles as they drifted forward, to the blast doors labeled 'Ballroom' towards the bow of the ship. It was then, as I followed several meters behind the Komeopians, that I realized the music I heard wasn't just playing in a far-off corner of my mind; it was playing from the grand ballroom at the front of the ship, down the hall to our right. That's where my Komeopian captors were all headed. They seemed in no hurry at all. Judging by their relaxed expressions, they needed a soak in something to relieve their usually wet bodies. With the rising humidity, the dim blue lighting, and the rushing waterfall, the hallway there on Deck B felt like some enchanted cybertech lagoon, where a river of dreams ran through a forest of pipes and gadgets.

Dreadnought waited, bobbing in the water lazily

as the music echoed to us from the ballroom on the other side of the hallway blast doors.

Pappy, who was doggy-paddling water like a bird with a broken wing, tugged on my arm. At first, I thought he was steadying himself, for he was still coughing and trying to keep the water out of his mouth. When he nearly yanked my arm from its socket, that's when I realized he wanted my quiet attention. He pulled me under the water, which was well over our heads already. A status sign showed four lifeboat icons, two of which were lit up green, with a green arrow underneath, pointed at the sealed ballroom doors.

Once I turned back to him, my hair trailing around me in the water, I nodded in understanding. I pointed from myself to him, indicating both of us.

Pappy shook his head 'no' and pointed at me. I felt the repulsion at this thought wrinkle my brow. He was not about to save me in some heroic gesture. I'd rescue him. I was surprised by the sentiment. Despite his piss-poor judgement with the Komeopian mutiny, I still felt Pappy was the closest thing to a friend I had found in recent years. He was a true survival ally, and we were trauma-bonding. Besides, my mind taunted, he was the only air-sucker I had left.

Sound moved slowly to me as I processed every second underwater like its own drawn-out minute. An ominous metal groan muttered forth from the elevator doors, where a Komeopian I didn't recognize by name had opened the doors to Lift 2. The current swept me away from Pappy's grasp, knocking me lightly against the ballroom doors. The pressure in the flooded hallway shifted yet again. Noting I was only a meter or so from the ceiling, I crashed through the surface of the water again, allowing myself to savor several deep breaths. My lungs were stinging as the fumes from that liquid hissed and fizzled around me.

Finally, I was ready to submerge again. Below me, Dreadnought was waving his clearance device over the panel lockscreen, and the thick metal blast doors to the ballroom were sliding open lazily.

I felt an undercurrent form once more, grabbing my ankles and sweeping me away from the surface of the water where it was safe to take a breath. My clothes felt heavier than ever, and I knew I could not fight against them. Under I went, my heart fluttering with panic, urging me to scream. I stayed focused. The water was sweeping me towards the opening formed by the Ballroom blast doors. They had only parted two meters, halted by a new set of sirens and blinking red hazard lights inside. In full surrender to the power of the water, I slipped through the doorway. Pappy sputtered at me, shouting out in surprise as we were both swept forward with room to breathe. And so, our mutinous party of pests was swallowed by the grand ballroom's hungry maw.

14. SHOCK AND AWE

"Step out of the water with your hands up!" The voice was familiar to me, calling out from my left. It was a Terran man.

I did as instructed, turning to my left where three crouching figures stood on the purple velvet carpet of a side stairwell. I took a few steps to them, using my forearm to move my hair out of my eyes as I raised my arms in compliance.

The stairs were built next to a stage with a traditional proscenium. A band of four robot musicians plucked away precisely at the string instruments in their quartet. The water rushing in was lapping at broken chairs and tables. Odd. Some awful riot must have occurred, for I had to step over more than one well-dressed corpse.

With a few intentional blinks, I tried to clear the water that still trickled down from my sopping wet hair and obstructed my view. Whoever was aiming an unlit shock-stick at me, they had a Deck Officer's hat. "Ms. Galikor, is that you?" It was First Officer Graves. In disbelief, I saw him lower his weapon.

I put my hands down.

The severe man rushed down the stairs to me as I staggered forward. My hopes stirred for the first time all night; more survivors!

"I must admit, I never thought I'd be so happy to see you," I said innocently to Officer Graves as I staggered forward. My legs were sore, weak from getting knocked around underwater, from kicking through the current.

"Likewise," Graves chuckled. "We thought you were the damned mutineers."

"About that," I said reluctantly. I was so relieved to see a familiar face, I'd nearly forgotten. "I'm not alone. The mutineers, they're–"

"Run for it," Pappy's voice rang out behind me over the roaring waterfall. The old man was ghost-white, splashing through the ankle-high water. His face was heavy with exhaustion, but his eyes were wild and wide, like some crazed feral animal. "They're right behind us!"

The alarms honked once more, then stopped. The blast doors groaned, no doubt from damming the water in the hallway, then they slid open harshly on their tracks.

Graves peered over my shoulder, took me firmly by the arm, and pulled me up the stairs past him. As he called out for Pappy to come to the stairs, I was greeted on the landing by a young man all buttoned up in his Security Officer's uniform, and a wrinkly greenish grey Fallamon in a top hat, coattails, and a monocle. Like a true gentle, the meter-tall reptile removed his hat and bowed to me. "Duke Frowl, at your service, mum," he croaked at me. The shell on his back was obscured under his custom-sewn matte satin coattails. The soldier did nothing. He let one hand hover over his holstered shock-stick.

Before I ducked out of sight on the stairs, the ballroom doors grumbled as they opened wider. The barnacled hides of Dreadnought's shiver toppled out with the next cascade of water. Graves backed out of their view, joining us up on the landing. I couldn't see anything, so I crept up the remaining stairs, which opened out onto a balcony level that framed the ballroom dance floor.

Graves crouched at the top of the stairs, his ragtag crew of survivors flanking him. 'What's going on,' he mouthed to me.

I shrugged and shook my head, holding a finger to my lips. Though they were clearly skeptical of me, Graves and his men seemed willing to wait and listen.

The string quartet struck up a vigorous tune as I heard Dreadnought's awful voice issue forth. "Where are my pet air-suckers?"

I crept along the shadows of the balcony, situating myself over the lip of the stage in time to see Pappy splashing back to Dreadnought.

"Here, m'boy! I'm here."

"Were you trying to get away?"

"Nh-no," Pappy said with a rattly, bone-aching cough. "Just needed a break from the water."

"Because you are weak," Dreadnought scolded. "You are made of water! Seventy percent! And yet it does you in. A walking contradiction, you apes!"

The other Komeopians were gathering in the doorway, flopping out on the floor and standing up like some undead army of spiny sea urchins.

"Where is my scribe," Dreadnought asked. "I wish for her to record something."

"Well, that's the tricky thing," Pappy said. We had crept up to the second level. I saw Pappy shake his head through the white wooden poles of the balcony's banister. "I think she ran out on us."

Graves raised a long, severe and well-groomed eyebrow at me. He shifted awkwardly. For a split second, I thought he might reach out and detain me. Thankfully, he did not. His partners seemed disappointed in his decision.

"You said she could be trusted," Dreadnought shouted.

"And I thought she could," Pappy spat the words back in retort. "Maybe she realized what a goddamned brat you are and figured she stood a better chance of survival running for a lifeboat!"

As Pappy waded through the knee-high water back to Dreadnought, the prickly brute curled up, hugging his knees. He sneered as Pappy approached.

"Chris'sake, Dread," the old sailor went on, "look what you've done to yourself. This whole damn escapade's been one big, rotten temper tantrum. As bad, if not worse, than the day I found you."

"You think I have not changed?"

"I do, I just… shit." Pappy took out his flask, popped the cap and tilted it back. "Frankly, because of your behavior, I been embarrassed more than anything. Your bad behavior drives me to drink!"

"You have never needed my help finding a reason to drink," Dreadnought snarled back.

"Hey, I *was* sober for years before I found you. This whole predicament has been bad for my nerves."

Dreadnought sucked in a short, angry breath. The big beast's right hand, which Pappy could not see from where he stood, dropped down to the shock-stick on his belt. He grabbed it, unclipped it from his belt, and swung it down hard at Pappy.

I had to stifle a cry as the bright blue wand of electricity crashed down into the water between them. A fountain of hot sapphire voltage sparked cracking between them like lightning. The man Pappy and his pupil Dreadnought were hurled apart as the shock-stick splintered to pieces.

The other Komeopians in the room clamored as far away from the scene as possible. Dreadnought propped himself up on his knees and webbed hands. He stood woozily, rocking like a drunken sailor. "Get up, Professor," Dreadnought barked.

He groped his way over to Pappy and shook him.

The old man's body splashed stiffly in the water. He was face-down in the pool, and I was fairly sure he wasn't breathing.

Dreadnought knelt before him, his face drooping like a pouting child. His scaly brow was beaded with water. In that moment, I saw his frailty. That face told me the truth; Dreadnought was just a scared, lost child.

The sad, wailing cry Dreadnought let out next told me for certain that Pappy was gone. "So that's it? You die on me when I need you most? You frail old creature!"

The Komeopians circled in around their leader and mimicked his cries. I turned to Graves at the top of the stairwell. He had wrinkles carved so deeply in his forehead; I thought his face might never truly recover.

Duke Frowl loosened his bowtie.

The Security Officer rolled his eyes.

Officer Graves straightened up, signaling all three of us to move out. We crept low along the wall, as far away from the balcony's edge as possible.

Dreadnought's sadness turned sour below us. We were working our way across the balcony to an emergency stairwell on the opposite end of the long dance floor, and we had to stop to hear what was being said.

"Sire, please put down the hurt stick," a Komeopian shouted desperately. "Your anger will hurt us again!" I cautioned a peek; it was Gunwale, the dark green Komeopian with frosty blue eyes. Kelp cowered

161

behind him.

"Do not question me," Dreadnought roared, swinging a new shock-stick. His subjects scrambled away from him. My new allies were creeping along the wall again, unconcerned with the piranha politics playing out before us in dramatic fashion.

The young security officer reached the doors to the emergency stairwell first. He stood guard, waiting as Officer Graves and Duke Frowl caught up and slipped through the door one at a time. I, however, continued to eavesdrop on Dreadnought as I brought up the rear. As his tirade ran on, I caught sight of Kelp crawling on all fours to Pappy's lifeless side.

He stretched out a quivering claw and gently caressed Pappy's weatherworn cheek, once flushed with a rosy hue from his persistent drinking, now pale and glossy as cold wax. My gaze wandered to Kelp's eyes and, for the first time, those dull, yellow globes, ever vacant, were now transformed into deep pools of endless sorrow. The only being who had ever given him a kindly word, an affectionate pat, or a warm smile was beyond his reach forever.

Dreadnought's rant rose again in its familiar petulant tone. "Do you see what has happened," he was preaching as I hustled to the door. "The scribe! This was her doing. Ever since the Professor brought her along, she's done nothing but sew distrust. She made the Professor doubt me, and now, his doubt poisons the trust of our shiver!" Dreadnought was singing through his tears like some damned crusader as he found new purpose for the destructive force of his shiver.

"We must not faulter. Search the ship! Find the scribe and bring her to me!"

I heard Dreadnought's orders plain as day, even over the jittering band and the rushing water. The security officer caught my eye as I slipped past him into the emergency stairwell, and I knew he had heard it, too.

15. ONE WAY OUT

July 9th, A.D. 2299
03:49 IST

"Quickly, sir," the security officer said to Graves as he eased the bar-latch shut quietly behind us. "They're on the move." That was it. No one said anything about what we had heard – what the Komeopians were suddenly after. The security officer did, however, continue to stare at me out of the corner of his eye like some self-assured surveillance camera.

My new party was light on their feet, and we had managed to slink stealthily to the landing down on Deck C when the clattering sound of the Deck B doors opening echoed through the stairwell above. I distinctly heard the wet, smacking sound of flippered feet slapping the metal landing directly above us. Water dripped and drizzled to us from above as it seeped out the door and down through the catwalk grates.

Graves stopped, deftly cracking the door to Deck C open with the stealth of a cat burglar. He waved us through and slipped in behind us. Methodically, Graves eased the door closed, then scanned the pipes and valves around us with his eyes.

"A-ha," he said mostly to himself as he grabbed a coil of chain hanging from a pipe and tangled it up in the door handles for the stairwell. As he stepped back to admire his work, the doors shook, and the chain rattled. I jumped, stifling a cry as something thumped the stairwell doors again, and the chain continued to swing.

"That'll hold 'em," Graves said affirmingly. He turned, waving us down the hallway.

"Hold on," I said rather insistently, "but where are we headed?"

"A fair question," Graves said with a slight bow. "I am leading us below decks because the ship is flooding from the top down." He spoke plainly, as though giving a damage report to a superior. "I know every crucial alert noise programmed into this ship's systems. I heard the alarm before it cut out. Those bastards drained the backup coolant tanks. Just popped the seals, changed the pressure, and whoosh!" Graves made a sweeping motion with his right hand. As he did, his hand led my gaze down the luxurious main hallway, where the cathedral-like ceilings matched those I had encountered on Deck B during boarding. That felt like a different trip, I realized. Somehow, it had happened to me a lifetime ago.

Deck C was strangely untouched. Nothing was in tatters, there were no corpses gestating Komeopian eggs in the hallway. It was eerily quiet, and our whole party was steeped in ominous shadows cast by the grand architecture under the blue nighttime running lights.

"I'm devoted to seeing all four of us safely off this waterlogged wreck," Graves reassured us with a nod. "But we really should press on," he urged.

At that, we wandered down the grand hallway of Deck C. We passed several elevator lifts, many of which had puddles forming at the seams of the doors. Other than the sing-song sound of pattering waterdrops dribbling from the ceiling, Deck C remained ominously silent.

I walked alongside Officer Graves as we made our way amidships. "I'm still trying to understand what they did to flood the ship," I pressed. "You said something about backup coolant tanks?"

"*Ichthus* has a massive engine," Graves said with a shrug. "The damn thing always runs hot. Only way to keep it running smoothly was to submerge the system in a coolant tank, rather than radiating the heat in phases. And because the damn liquid vaporizes as the engines burn hot, the designers had to figure out a way to keep extra coolant on-hand for these long voyages. With the artificial gravity generator working, it's easier... and cheaper... to store that extra coolant above the engines and siphon it down as needed. Water runs downhill, as the saying goes."

"Oh, of course," I said, realizing finally what he was driving at. "The smokestacks?"

"Aye," Graves said, snapping to attention. "The smokestacks. More accurately, auxiliary coolant tanks."

"Ah," I said, piecing things together. "The lower we go, the dryer it gets?"

"For the time being," said Graves severely.

"What about the lifeboats up on Deck B," I asked.

"Sabotage," Graves muttered.

"We lost a good soldier," The security officer sighed melodramatically.

"And several brave passengers," Duke Frowl croaked sadly.

Our party of four ducked down another long hallway, then Graves steered us into a food court. "There was no lifeboat," Graves said, shaking his head, "just a group of rogue deck concierges with a hacker among them." He opened his arms to the food court before us. "Gather up some rations," he instructed. You'll thank me when you see the freeze-dried alternative aboard these efficiency-class lifeboats." He paused, procuring tote bags from a souvenir rack behind him and began vigorously stuffing those with food.

"So, these rogues hacked the lifeboats," I urged Graves for the rest of his story.

"Not exactly," Graves went on, his long arms plucking up granola like a grasshopper gathering wheat. "They hacked the signage on Deck B to make it appear as though there were still two lifeboats left. In reality, there were none. I had a team of eight survivors when we showed up to that damned emergency bay, including the duke here," he gestured to the Fallamon in coattails. The short reptile was plucking a variety of fruits from a nearby health stand. "When we rounded the corner to the lifeboats, those rogues cut off our exit and demanded our valuables."

The security officer shook his head, his chin jutting at the air around him as his mouth contorted in disgust. "Survival situation with your fellow man, and all you care about is profit."

"I absolutely agree," Graves nodded. "They're… disappointing, to say the least."

"They're parasites!" The security officer's neck turned pink, a vein throbbing with his proclamation.

Graves patted him on the back. He demonstrated a deep breath, emphasized by the flourishing of a long arm. "Breathe, Corporal Blake. It's important to remain calm in these situations." Graves was so relaxed, so methodical; it was impressive. "They lied about having two lifeboats, so we bartered passage with valuables and promises. When we caught on about the missing boats and protested to their scam, they overpowered us."

"The three of us managed to fall back as far as the ballroom. By then, the flood had started. Before I lost data on the ship's systems, the aft lifeboat bay on Deck E still had three lifeboats remaining."

"What of you," Duke Frowl prodded somewhat playfully. "How did you come to us?"

I thought for a moment. How did I explain what I had agreed to? If I told them I'd partnered with Pappy to survive, I faced an uncomfortable and scrutinous time aboard our lifeboat… I would just limit the truth as I needed to for survival, I resolved. It was threatening to become a theme of my *Ichthus* experience. "The Komeopians discovered I was a writer and kidnapped me. They kept talking about liberating themselves—"

"Codswallop," Graves interjected scornfully.

"How do you know what they call themselves," Corporal Blake asked. He stepped towards me, and his pupils flashed with intense scrutiny.

Graves put a hand up in front of the young man.

"I, uh…"

"I'll save you the trouble of another lie," Blake barked. "Officer Graves, sir, those things are looking for her."

Graves's right eyebrow bent instantly to a point as he examined me. "That's a bold claim," he said. "What makes you think this?"

"I overheard them," Blake said, taking an empty tote of food from Graves and stocking it with supplies. He watched me the whole time, like a foe at the card table searching for my bluff.

Graves cleared his throat. "I must admit, I thought I heard them blathering on about you," he said to me.

"They wanted me to write about them," I confessed.

"Why," Duke Frowl's voice cracked with

169

curiosity.

"They were founding their own new history... they were going to make me write it for them."

Graves adjusted his hat, hefting tote bags of food over his shoulders. "Good luck," he scoffed.

"And why did they want you, specifically?" Young Corporal Blake was condescending, to say the least.

I responded as plainly as possible. "Because I'm a travel journalist."

Graves put a hand on my shoulder. "I can verify that."

Blake's chin extended proudly again. He nodded to himself like he'd caught a child in a lie. "And how would they know you're a writer unless you conspired with them somehow?"

"I had the unfortunate pleasure of crossing paths with the old drunkard Artemis Bounty." I felt bad belittling him, especially so soon after he... but then, what could I do? "I met him in one of the onboard bars–"

"Sounds like him," Blake snarked.

"I thought his career travels might make for a good human-interest piece." I waited a moment as Blake considered all this, and I made damn sure to pack some food while carrying on with them.

"Okay, so fine," Blake offered. "She's got an answer for everything."

"The mark of truth," Graves suggested.

Blake sneered. "Mark of excuses, if you ask me," he muttered.

Graves shook his head. "What is your problem, soldier?"

"I don't trust her."

"I don't recall asking if you did." A flash of fierceness crossed Graves's eyes.

"I told you I heard the goddamned fish people when we were leaving the ballroom. They're searching the whole ship *to find her*! Just leave her behind and they won't even know the rest of us are here."

"Have you no decency?" Graves had more color in his face than I thought possible.

"Everyone else is talking," Blake shrugged. "I should have a say, too."

"A say in whether or not she survives," Graves asked with bewilderment. "Listen to yourself, man!"

"Better than listening to *you*," Blake scolded. "You're liable to get us all killed playing hero."

"Corporal Blake, this is a survival situation. We are still aboard our vessel, and I am your superior officer. Any and all persons I encounter who prove to be better than common scoundrels, be they Cliptorgian, Hulgarian, human or otherwise, will accompany us back to civilization in a lifeboat." He was cool and exacting in his assertion.

"Are you actually pulling rank on me right now? Do you think that matters? This is survival, now. This is fighting tooth and claw! We should all have a fair say, or we should fend for ourselves." Blake's hand hovered over the shock-stick holstered on his belt. Graves shoved a tote bag full of supplies into the young man's arms. "Fine. It's democracy then. Duke, would you care to weigh in?"

The Fallamon regarded all three of us. Gently, his soft, scaly fingers tugged at my hand, urging me to kneel to his height. I did so, and he sniffed the air around my face. "Is what you tell us true? Did the beasts force you into servitude?"

"Yes," I said. "I was given an ultimatum," I added. I'd seen the duke's tactic used before in my journeys. Fallamon claimed that they could tell whether or not a mammal was lying because our perspiration smelled different when employing deception. A full statement like mine would no doubt convince him.

Duke Frowl peered past me, up at Graves and Blake. "I trust her," he said, releasing my hand with a flourish of his own.

"That settles it," Graves said. "Ms. Galikor, I do hope this means you're joining us. We really must get moving now." He hoisted four totes of food, then made a quarter-turn on his heeled boot. "As many bags as you can carry," he said. We obeyed.

Officer Graves nodded decisively. "This way," he coaxed, and our quartet dashed for a nearby emergency stairwell.

Blake held the door for everyone. Panic fluttered in my chest as Graves and the duke marched through the door first. Blake shot me a warning look as I approached him. 'I'm watching you,' he mouthed at me.

I shifted to duck past him, and felt the familiar

bump of my pistol move ever so slightly under my tunic. A confidence settled over me as Blake shut the door behind us. I was still armed...

16. LIFEBOAT 16

July 9th, A.D. 2299
04:12 IST

Water had started drizzling down on us from the decks above like an inconsistent rain. The sound of those drops plunked off everything, amplified like raindrops in old catacombs. The ambiance gave our own sounds some cover, so we kept moving through that dimly lit tower of egress.

Finally, we reached the bottom of the stairwell. The sign over the stairs read 'Deck E' in friendly green letters, and a puddle rippled on the metal floor, disturbed by the steady stream of water tumbling down from the upper decks.

Slowly, Graves slipped his hand into the door handle and eased it open, ushering us out into a hallway much like the one where my cabin could be found. We turned left, heading towards stern.

Graves pointed to a physical sign at the end of the hallway, about eight meters away. I couldn't believe my weary eyes. It read, 'Aft Lifeboat Bay E.' The blue emergency lighting made the silver plaque's letters seem to glow on the wall.

My heart skipped a beat; we were so close, there was signage! Even if we got separated, I'd be able to find my way. And I doubted any of them would take their chances in a lifeboat alone. It wasn't my preference either, but it meant that either alone or with these three oddballs, I was going to survive. The tightness in my chest loosened just a bit with my next breath.

We covered ten meters, all of it cramped lower deck lodgings. In the dark, I pondered all the dead passengers. How many doors in this hallway represented casualties? The E Deck cabin doors stared back at me like old tombstones through the gates of a graveyard at night. Thankfully, the hallway opened wider to accommodate a set of passenger lifts.

The seams along the elevator doors spat rivulets of water, misting the cool, stale air around us. We moved beyond the lifts, and I recognized the doorway into Aft Dining Hall E, where I had dined on the first night of the voyage. Involuntarily, my gaze fell upon the tank in the court's far corner where I had first seen the infernal eyes of a Komeopian.

A chill ran down my spine: the piping.

Why hadn't I thought of it sooner? We were traipsing along these hallways, ducking around corners like detectives, yet none of us were watching the pipes! Grimtash.

Despite my urge not to look, I raised my head to peer at the copper tubing overhead. The greenish liquid still churned through them. I tapped Graves on the shoulder. "When they first found me, they were using the piping to travel around the ship," I advised.

He stopped. "Really?" Graves chewed on his lower lip as he processed the information. "And they can fit?"

"They seem to come in a variety of sizes," I said. "The smaller ones definitely fit."

"That's how they did it," Graves muttered to himself. "The passenger decks were supposed to be off limits." His shoulders drooped. "C'mon, this way," he said for our benefit.

Blake switched on a flashlight and kept it pointed at the pipes above us as we continued down the corridor, guided by the beacon of that silver lifeboat signage in its ethereal indigo spotlight.

"There," Duke Frowl exclaimed, his clawed grey finger pointing up as we passed a connecting hallway off to our left. A dark, glistening lump with a spiked crown was lingering in a spherical glass protuberance not three meters from us. It was one of them. Its dull, wide-set eyes seemed familiar.

Then, the Komeopian blinked lazily, one eye and then the other: Kelp. He smiled as the beam from Blake's flashlight washed over his face. In the pale, revealing light I could see all the puckered scars that covered Kelp's arms, neck and shoulders.

"Double-time," Graves said, gently pushing us onward. Before Blake's flashlight moved off him, Kelp zipped away around an elbow in his pipe, no doubt searching for a way to cut us off.

"What if he follows us," Blake asked.

"No doubt he already is," Graves said. "But the nearest access door for pipe maintenance will spit him out further away from us."

"You seem awful confident," I said.

Graves shrugged. "Rule number one for any officer worth his salt: know your ship."

We reached the signage at the end of the hall and ducked ahead into the portside lifeboat bay. Three steps down, and we spilled out into a relatively small room with ceilings so high, I could not discern them in the sad, dim emergency running lights.

Black catwalks stretched only three meters before us, and the width couldn't have been more than one meter. To our left, there were three circular hatches at ground level. A set of black metal stairs at the far end of the bay led up to a catwalk offering access to three more hatches. Through the catwalk grating we stood on, I could see a third level below us. On our own level, all three hatches were already shut tight and sealed off. The hatches were labeled Lifeboat 08, Lifeboat 10, and Lifeboat 12 in white block lettering on the matte black metal frame around each circular door. A little red light next to each of the thick doors read 'Lifeboat Deployed.'

I peered through the grating and distinctly saw a green status light next to one of the hatches below us. "There," I urged them, "below us."

We hustled to the stairwell, descending as quickly as possible without toppling over each other. Blake was at the bottom first. As soon as he hit the ground, we heard Blake say, "Ah, shit."

We stopped in our tracks, Graves and I still two stairs from the bottom. There was Kelp, standing in the shadowy center hatch labeled 'Lifeboat 16.' He was dripping wet still from his swim through the pipes, and the smell of boggy sea air lingered.

"Knew you would come," he said with an exaggerated, jittery nod. It was the kind of full body nod I'd seen exotic birds do. He held out his arms to bar our passage to the lifeboat. I found his wingspan was abnormally long for his short stature. He pointed at me. "To lifeboats... to freedom," he asked, stepping in front of the green status light of Lifeboat 16.

Perhaps he was brighter than he seemed, I thought.

Blake unclipped his shock-stick from his belt and extended it. The tip sizzled with hot blue electricity.

"Kelp does not want fight," the Komeopian pleaded, his voice cooing. Then, it got deep and guttural, "but verse you Kelp will win."

"Perhaps," Graves said, taking the last few stairs and positioning himself between Blake and Kelp. Graves pulled his own shock-stick. "But perhaps not."

Kelp shrieked, throwing his hands crisply into the

air again. The sound echoed up through the lifeboat bay, bouncing back to us like some phantom in the rafters.

"Kelp no want fight. Kelp want freedom!"

"If you're saying you want to come with us," Blake snapped, "you can forget it."

"Kelp? Was that you?" The voice was low and distant, but it was unmistakably Dreadnought's. And it sounded like it was coming to us from somewhere else on Deck E.

Kelp shot us all a panicked look. Then, he shushed us. "Hide, quick! Kelp will help."

Fortunately, The *Ichthus* was consistent in its design, and there were solid black pipes woven all around the lifeboat bay, closing it in with imperfect mechanical walls. We all scattered without thinking. Duke Frowl dropped to the floor and swung himself under the bottom of the stairwell. His black tuxedo blended nicely into the shadows.

Graves found a gap between two vertical pipes, sucked in his slight belly, and squeezed himself between them.

Blake was gone before I saw what he did, but I took my tote of extra food supplies, found a horizontal pipe running parallel to the floor, and rolled myself under it as I had done with Pappy when we hid from his coworker.

Kelp stood in the middle of the room, squinting at where we had gone. He seemed to nod nervously to himself.

"Kelp," it was Dreadnought, and he was much, much closer. "Are you in here?"

Even though I was in hiding, I realized I felt exposed. For some damn reason, I had gone into hiding on my back. It was a terribly vulnerable feeling that suddenly made my nerves leap. They pounded at my chest. Clinging to the shadows, I realized I could lean ever so slightly and peer up through the catwalk grating to see what was going on.

Dreadnought appeared on the catwalks above us. I hate to say I recognized his particular stench, but I did. Whereas the whole shiver smelled of seaweed and shore-bog, Dreadnought also stunk of fetid meat, like some wild carnivore. His wet, webbed feet slapped the catwalk as he moved towards the stairwell.

Kelp rushed to meet him. "Yes, sire. Coming, sire!"

"You *are* here," Dreadnought asked. He seemed to lean forward, likely trying to discern more in the darkness. He crossed the catwalks above us, and I held my breath. I didn't want to utter the slightest whisper.

Dreadnought stopped at the top of the stairs. "Have you found anything?" He sniffed the air.

"No, sire. Disappointment, sire." Kelp scrambled up the stairs. Impressive, I thought. He was trying to keep Dreadnought away from us. My mind raced. What had Kelp said when we found him?

He said he wanted freedom. Did he want to join us in the lifeboat? Could my allies tolerate such a thing? That likely relied upon how much they knew about the

Komeopian reproduction process. I cringed, remembering that visceral scene. Knowing what I did, could I tolerate such a thing, I wondered.

On the other hand, Kelp struck me more and more like an abused puppy. He was meek and mild, especially compared to the rest of his ilk.

Dreadnought gave a melancholy sigh. "She will come," he said, his shoulders slouching as he turned back. Then, as he crossed the catwalk over top of my position, he stopped, digging for something in the pouch he had tied to his belt. Careful to keep my face in the darkest shadows, I leaned my head to the right to get a better view. Dreadnought lifted the melon-sized thing in front of his face to behold it at arm's length. As he did so, water dripped down through the grate, pattering the floor right next to me. Another drop landed in my right eye. I tried to blink it away, but it clouded my vision. I kept that eye shut.

Dreadnought was still talking. "He would have told us to look to the lifeboats. How such wisdom used to pass through these lips, now cold and lifeless." Dreadnought chuckled to himself. "Where be your gibes now? Your gambols? Your songs?" The wet melon in his hand found a small spotlight as he moved it, revealing the awful truth to me: it was Pappy's severed head.

I saw another drop of crimson spatter on the grating above and realized what was in my eye. Blood. More specifically, blood from Pappy's head, which Dreadnought held aloft like Yorick's skull in his own cheap rendition of *Hamlet*.

Shuddering, I ducked my head back into hiding, frantically wiping the blood from my eye as Dreadnought carried on. "Your flashes of merriment, that were want to set the table on a roar? Not one now to mock your own grinning." Dreadnought laughed again, a stuttering sound that seemed to shatter as he burst into tears. He wailed, tucking Pappy's head back in its cloth pouch, where it hung lazily from his massively muscular outer thigh.

I heard Kelp laugh awkwardly. "Sire likes the fancy language."

It was all so absurdly strange. I couldn't help but shake my head.

Dreadnought stifled his tears, altering his unmistakable wail of agonizing grief into a choking cough. I leaned out again so I could see.

He cleared his throat and shook his head. "Not a word of this," he snapped at Kelp.

Kelp said nothing, but did something I have only ever seen Terrans do... he pinched his index finger and thumb together and ran them across his lips to indicate closing a zipper. I had no doubt he'd learned that from Pappy. Which meant he understood its meaning. He certainly used it in the right context.

"Stay here," Dreadnought hissed. "Hide in the shadows. When she comes for a lifeboat, bring her to me."

"Aye, aye, sir," Kelp said with a salute.

Nodding sharply, Dreadnought ducked out of the

room, his wet cape thwacking the door frame as he rushed the three steps up out of the lifeboat bay.

The split-second Dreadnought was out, my peripheral caught movement. It was Blake. Before any of us could react, the short-tempered security officer leapt from his hiding spot and rolled into the circular hatch to Lifeboat 16. Kelp rushed back down the stairs, but I knew he hadn't seen Blake.

I slid out of hiding as quickly as I could, rolled over onto my hands and knees, and pulled my pistol from my tunic. I was not about to let Blake take the lifeboat himself, and I didn't trust him enough to risk further setbacks. If I intended to survive, it was now or never.

My mind raced. I would have to act fast, be assertive, and take control of the situation. I also had to be willing to shoot him if he didn't cooperate. For that to be safe, I would have to be close.

As I crossed the catwalks, Hatch 16 shined back at me, a circular beacon of salvation in that dim, dark docking bay.

Still, my thoughts raced, far outpacing real time. Larger lifeboats required at least two people to operate the helm smoothly, designed intentionally that way to deter deserters. That didn't stop the occasional overconfident hothead from trying on his own. "Going TOMS," a sailor once called it. Naturally, I had asked him to elaborate. TOMS, he had explained, was an acronym for 'The One-man Moon Shot,' an old expression of luck. Corporal Blake definitely struck me as the type who might end up going TOMS.

I climbed through the hatch and into the accordion rubber of the lifeboat's docking umbilicus. The short tunnel wiggled and wobbled around me, the illusion dizzying to my eyes as I tried to hold my pistol steady.

I didn't hear anything as I approached the hatch into Lifeboat 16. The nerve I had to muster to hold the pistol steady urged me to confront Blake quicker. Intuition, however, told me to stop. I held back.

Around me, it was suspiciously silent. Noise from behind me drew my attention. The others had squeezed out of their hiding spots and were making their way towards us. As their footsteps drew near, Blake got bored. He sprung into view from the left, his shock-stick sizzling at me. The rage he had mustered into his face cooled instantly as he comprehended my pistol aimed right at his heart.

"Going somewhere," I asked threateningly. I was trying to keep my voice down.

"You bitch," he hissed.

"Ms. Galikor," Graves exclaimed behind me as he rushed to the hatch and saw only my outstretched hands pointing my pistol.

"Blake here seems to be going TOMS on us, Officer Graves." I spoke the words over my left shoulder to him, but my eyes stayed locked on Blake's.

"What are you doing," Blake tried appealing to me. He was shouting. "You heard that thing: it wants to come with us."

"Keep your voice down," I ordered him. I must admit, I was impressed with my voice's note of authority.

Duke Frowl rushed to my side, his head barely clearing my waist. He growled when he saw Blake in the doorway.

"Keep it down," Frowl warned, "before you bring that big bastard back."

Graves climbed into the umbilicus. Kelp was hot on his trail, slithering in behind him. I saw Kelp crouch down, leaning to see around his legs. "Officer Blake," Graves said, his voice leveled with reason. "It would be much safer if you let us all aboard."

"Leave the fish," Blake ordered them.

"Kelp not bad," Kelp pleaded behind Graves. He tried pushing forward, but Graves stepped into his way.

"Hold on, now," the First Officer said to Kelp. "We should discuss terms."

"Any terms," Kelp urged. "Any terms!"

"Drop the gun," Blake snapped at me.

I decided to try my luck before our commotion drew another Komeopian to us. Narrowing my brow at Blake, I took a step forward.

He raised his hands and backpedaled deeper into the lifeboat.

I took another step.

Blake backed up again.

"Duke Frowl, clear the door for Graves," I said, keeping the pistol trained on Blake. Duke Frowl rolled forward, scrambling into Lifeboat 16 with us. He went straight for the helm.

My heart was pounding. How did I resolve this? Was I prepared to kill Blake to survive this mess? I thought about the corpses floating around in the upper decks. How many lives had been claimed by the flood? I remembered the other security officers who'd died at Dreadnought's hands. Blake didn't realize how lucky he'd been. He'd still be spared the awful fate of his team, even if I shot him. My pistol trained on him still, I ducked into the lifeboat myself.

Don't call my bluff, I begged him telepathically.

Graves appeared in the hatch behind me. Kelp was practically glued to his side. Graves seemed to notice, for I saw him do a doubletake as Kelp gripped his pant-leg.

"Get aboard, Officer Graves," I instructed.

"I told you we should have left this bitch," Blake snapped. He spoke around me at Graves, as though I wasn't in the room.

"Damn it, man; where's your humanity?" Graves pleaded.

Blake sneered at us all. "She's *not* human."

"That's not what I asked," Graves said, straightening up with an air of indignance.

Something roared behind me, followed by a sickeningly wet *thwack*, a warm mist of crimson, and Graves cried out in agony. My whole body flinched all at once, startled into a flurry of adrenaline. My trigger finger squeezed the pistol, and a burst of hot energy knocked me backwards.

The shot buried itself in Blake's chest, his eyes fixed on the hatch behind me. His last moments left his face contorted in a gasp of horror.

I caught my balance and turned, and only then did I realize the horror of Blake's last sight. Officer Graves had been cleaved in two vertically. Dreadnought's Cliptorgian broadsword had ripped through the man's shoulder and had traveled almost straight down to his waistline.

Dreadnought heaved in the umbilicus, his spiny shoulders threatening to puncture the inner layer of rubber. He glared at me, his body shaking in the fiercest guttural noise I had yet heard any of the Komeopians make. It rumbled through the lifeboat, shaking the core of my being with a primal, unreasonable, angry fear. I had never before, nor have I since felt such terrible shock.

Miraculously, Graves was alive and still standing. Though his body was split down the middle, his hands seemed to grab aimlessly at the room around him for stability. The crisp white collared undershirt of his uniform soaked through with blood in seconds, transformed to a deep crimson as the poor man gasped and grasped. He was in shock, for he said nothing, only choked for air.

Kelp had disappeared from sight.

Violently, Dreadnought shook his sword, trying to dislodge it from the mid-torso of poor First Officer Graves. Dreadnought lifted his foot and shoved

Graves away from him, yanking the sword free as he did. The broadsword came loose, and Officer Graves dropped to his knees.

Dreadnought ducked, preparing to squeeze through the hatch. Graves was a step ahead of him, though, throwing his awkward weight into Dreadnought's legs. He tangled himself up as he lost his balance, and I distinctly saw his hands still grasping at the Komeopian's knees. Dreadnought tripped, falling to the floor. He growled, swiping at Graves with his claws.

Just then, my eyes darted to Kelp. He reappeared behind the scene of carnage, in the accordion rubber tunnel of the umbilicus that tethered our lifeboat to the starship. I half expected to see him trembling and cowering at Dreadnought's massive bulk. Yet that was not the case. Kelp was trembling, but it wasn't from fear. A hoarse mewl sputtered from his lips, a cry of determination rather than dismay. Then, the slight Komeopian uttered forth a rage-filled howl that grew from the depths of his vitals and escaped through gritted teeth. The sound erupted in a crescendo of pain, misery, and all the stinging agony suppressed through a lifetime of abuse.

Kelp lunged forward, leaping onto Dreadnought's back. The big brute was writhing on the ground, trying to toss the convulsing Graves from his own entangled legs. As Kelp leapt, he reached behind his back and produced an indigo orb from spaces unknown. I recognized it immediately. The tell-tale color and spindly black legs within meant it was a gut-skipper, no doubt ready for its morning meal.

Kelp wrapped an arm around Dreadnought's neck, using his wrist spines to anchor into his rampaging leader's chest. His other arm flailed wildly, maneuvering for the perfect angle at which to shove the gut-skipper orb down Dreadnought's gnashing jaws.

Dropping his sword with a sharp, metallic clatter and grabbing Kelp by what could be considered the scruff of his neck, Dreadnought vainly strove to toss his gangly subject up and over his stout shoulders. He flailed on the floor like a fish out of water. But the more he pulled and flexed, the deeper Kelp's spines dug, prompting sable rivulets of inky black blood to trickle down his muscular frame. With each tug, Dreadnought's growling gasps grew coarser and more labored, causing his gills to flare wider and wider.

Of course! I leaped forward toward the towering tangle of scales and fins. Time to test a theory. I jammed a firm, open hand between Dreadnought's flapping gills, scraping my knuckles against his spikey cartilage. This absolutely had the intended effect. As soon as my fingertips sank into the tender, fatty tissue of his gills, Dreadnought opened his mouth as wide as it would go, trying to gulp for a breath of water. Kelp saw his chance and rammed the gut-skipper orb as far down Dread's gullet as it would go.

Instinctively, Dreadnought swallowed hard to try to clear his breath-ways, and in so doing condemned himself to a horrible end. Kelp dislodged his wrists and sprang back down to the floor.

The duke and I were both frozen in place. We stood at the ready, just out of reach of the maelstrom of Komeopian limbs in the hatch door, but our intervention was unnecessary. I considered my pistol, then instantly shut the idea down. My target was too far, and only an umbilicus separated us from the vacuum of space. One misfire, and I'd kill us all.

Dreadnought staggered back, grasping at his torso with jittering flippers. "What have you done, Kelp? What have you done!" Dreadnought wailed, rolling on his back, twisting and jerking this way and that. "You," he thundered, pointing the stub of his severed right index finger at me, "You turned him against me!"

"That was your own doing."

"Kelp! Help, help me," Dreadnought implored.

Kelp remained as still as stone, crouched in a corner of the lifeboat, just beyond Dreadnought's reach.

"I said help, you runt! You *minimus*!"

At that, Kelp rose to his feet, so swiftly and in such a fluid motion, even Dreadnought flinched in surprise. Then, he pounced on Dreadnought's stomach.

"Weak," Kelp demanded indignantly, towering over his prey, "Weak?! No! Kelp is strong. Kelp has thrown down mighty Dreadnought!" Kelp leaned in. "Kelp claims Angwari on your soul." He purred these last words as he relished his revenge.

Dreadnought's bewildered expression turned

suddenly to one of utter amusement. "Angwari," he scoffed, "You cannot claim Angwari. You are the runt of the shiver." He did his best to chuckle as the gut-skipper began its gruesome work.

"No," Kelp screeched, then sank his claws into Dreadnought's eyes. The big beast cried out in such shrill agony, I knew at least one of his eyes had been mangled. I saw the gushing inky blood burst forth, dousing Kelp's arms and chest.

Dreadnought screamed in agony.

Holding a firm grip on his victim, Kelp turned maniacal. "Now Kelp is the one who pecks!" Abruptly Kelp froze, a sly, sinister grin spreading across his face. "But who does Kelp peck? Boatswain? No, Boatswain pecks others, several others. And Bowsprit? Some others. But never Boatswain." as Kelp continued, he paced behind his fallen commander. He snatched up the hilt of Dreadnought's broadsword, dragged it along behind him, making a shrill, grating sound as it glided on the floor. "And who does Gunwale peck at?" He paused dramatically. "Rudder," he answered himself cheerily. "And Kelp?"

He glowered at Dreadnought, who had stopped screaming and now sobbed, pleading on the floor. "Don't do this, Kelp," he sputtered through his pooling blood. I could see that his pearly, needlelike teeth were stained with it, as though a pen had burst while he chewed on the cap.

Kelp paused, allowing the moment to grow more tense. "Who does Kelp peck at?" He struggled slightly as he lifted the Cliptorgian broadsword over his head. Then, in a viciously victorious tone, Dreadnought's victim became his vanquisher. "Kelp pecks… at you."

Arching his back, Kelp swung the sword down hard on Dreadnought's face. With a sickening, wet smack, crunch, and hiss, the falling blade slammed down diagonally across Dreadnought's face. With a pitiful yelp and the slight kick of his legs, Dreadnought died before us. Kelp had missed his neck and instead sliced his tyrant's head apart just above the lower jaw.

None of us said a word as Dreadnought's body quaked and jolted with his final death spasms. All that could be heard was the sound of the sword's blade tip scraping the metal floor: a sharp ringing which, as the seconds passed, slowly waned until there was only the silent hum of the starship's distant engines.

Kelp landed on his rump, slumped over, as much in shock as the rest of us. He blinked: first the left eye, then the right. I sidled up to him, not wanting to agitate him further but knowing, even with Dreadnought's death, that each passing minute lessened our chances of escape.

"Kelp? We have to go," I urged softly. I wanted him to come with us. I wasn't about to quibble about it with Duke Frowl. Not with Blake dead behind me and Graves dying before me.

"Go," Kelp asked after a few short, wheezing breaths. "No, stay! We stay!" Desperately, he fell to his knees, retrieving Dreadnought's mallet-scepter from his belt. "Kelp lead now, by right of Angwari." He lifted the scepter and puffed out his chest.

Already I could see where this was going and, while I was not Komeopian, I had spent enough time with them to know this spontaneous delusion of grandeur would not work out the way Kelp hoped it would.

"But who would know," I asked, sweetening my voice. "Would any in your shiver believe you?" It felt cruel and heartless to say those words. After so many years of condescension and abuse from his fellow beings, was I any better to manipulate that in him? But I pushed those thoughts down and continued, "Who bore witness to it?"

Kelp thought for a moment, then pointed at me with a smile. "Scribe," he chirped excitedly. He spread his clawed flippers wide, holding them up at me in a gesture of surrender. "Scribe has witnessed it! Scribe and Shell," he persisted, pointing to the duke, who, admittedly, didn't seem too keen on Kelp's innocent nickname.

"And would they believe us? An air-sucker who betrayed the mighty Dreadnought? A Fallamon in finery?" I gestured to the duke. "...or Kelp. Would they believe you, Kelp?"

Kelp's mouth slackened a little, gravelly breaths whistling through his teeth, as my implications crept through his mind.

"Kelp claimed Angwari," he reiterated, weaker this time. "Kelp has claimed the head of Dreadnought."

"I know," I said, placing a hand on his shoulder. "But with the whole shiver pecking at Kelp, what if someone else claims Angwari on *you*?"

"But... but..." He stammered, struggling. "But... Kelp pecks now," he insisted. Yet that insistence had shrunk to little more than a whisper, and his voice cracked on the final word. He blinked: first the left eye, then the right.

"I know," I said, softer still.

Kelp's shoulders sank and his arms fell limp at his sides. It was then he fully understood; the life he had known, regardless of its brutality, was gone. It had been washed away like so many other things that night.

He blinked again: both eyes together. There was no going back. On wobbling limbs, Kelp crawled weakly onto one of the lifeboat's benches. He curled up, his glistening arms wrapped around his scaly legs.

Duke Frowl gently prodded me. "Madame, would you be so good as ta' help me clear this mess from the hatchway?

"Of course," I replied. "I'm sorry." I rose to my feet and beheld the bloody scene before me. Dreadnought's not-quite-headless corpse, stiff and cold, still spurted the occasional dribble of blood. His legs were blanketed by Graves' nearly bisected bulk. The First Officer's glassy eyes stared up at me from that gory vignette I still wish I could unsee.

We had to lean our backs against the support struts in the hatch doorway and use our feet to force Dreadnought's shoulders out of the hatch door. The rubber umbilicus connector wobbled as it took the rest of his weight.

Somewhere out in the hallway, I heard the commotion of flippered feet and wet fabric in the walkways above. "Here they come," I warned. Then, I spied a glowing red button to the left of the lifeboat's hatch. 'Emergency Lock' it glowed like an electric ruby. "Clear," I commanded, and I smacked that button so hard, the plastic bubble cap cracked a little.

As the hatch to Lifeboat 16 rumbled shut, I stayed focused. The duke and I nodded to each other and rushed to the steerage consoles at stern. The whole vessel spread out before us, and I felt a steadiness settle into my chest. I realized I was suddenly confident in my own survival. I breathed a sigh of relief. Finally.

Our consoles were scrolling through step-by-step instructions for how to activate the emergency escape vessel. We both rushed through the prompts onscreen, each of us dancing a nervous jig as we waited for each confirmation chime from our computers. Then, an alarm rang out and something beyond the hatch door hissed. "Launch procedures initiated," the lifeboat's onboard computer assistant greeted us. "Our sincere apologies for any inconvenience you've experienced today."

"You're still getting a bad review," I sassed the computer.

"Please stand by," the lifeboat's onboard system requested. After only a moment, the computer spoke again. "Your lifeboat is ready for takeoff."

A green button appeared on both of our steering consoles. "Please confirm together within five seconds." A countdown proceeded.

The duke and I nodded to each other, and, in perfect synchronicity, we tapped the green buttons before us. Then, the lifeboat lurched forward, released from its clamps and jettisoned away from the *Starship Ichthus*. I felt the lifeboat shift and shudder, escaping the gravity drag of the starliner, and I imagined we must look like a runaway comet, hurtling away like some pebble tossed into a sea of stars.

17. SAFE HARBOR

July 9th, A.D. 2299
06:01 IST

The three of us sat quietly in Lifeboat 16 for I don't know how long. The duke and I were at stern, where all the helm controls were located. Kelp hadn't moved from the bench he'd claimed before takeoff.

I had the distinct understanding in that soft, still silence that all three of us needed a moment of peace. So, we sat for a good long while. None of us seemed to look at the corpse of Corporal Blake sprawled awkwardly across the floor. That was something I wasn't sure how to unpack. On the one hand, I wanted to thank The Rings my shot had landed true in his chest, preserving the hull of the lifeboat around us. On the other hand, I'd directly added to the body count. Even worse, I'd brought the evidence with us in the lifeboat.

Duke Frowl was clearly reflecting on that tricky detail, too, for his next question gave it away. "What do we do with this poor bastard?"

"I haven't the slightest clue," I admitted.

Duke Frowl tapped the console nearest him at the helm. "We need a star chart. Does anyone have a damned clue how far out we sailed?"

"If we crossed the Barrier," I said, "we'd have known." Any cruise that made the effort to pass out of ISF space and into the Free Worlds of the Outer Rim made a huge show of it before turning back. When pirate activity was high in a given region, cruise ships received ISF military escorts. It added to the novelty of voyages through unregulated space.

"True," the duke agreed with me at first. Then, after another silent moment, he added, "Oh?" He was studying a readout on his steering console.

"What is it," I asked.

"We did cross the Barrier," he observed. "We've been sailing through unregulated space all night."

"Why didn't they make the announcement," I asked.

"Says here we crossed over just last night, at 22:14 Interstellar Standard Time."

"Maybe with all the departure delays, they didn't want to cause a commotion that late at night," I offered.

"Who cares," Duke Frowl shrugged. "The closer we are, the better. These smaller lifeboats don't move as fast. We'll probably be aboard for at least a full day's cycle." I had nothing to offer, so I just nodded to demonstrate my understanding.

The meter-tall Fallamon folded his spindly hands behind his back, resting them on a bump in his shell. He began pacing up and down the deck in front of me, clearly deep in thought. "My best contacts are in the Far Reaches," he explained. The Far Reaches were exactly what they sounded like: the farthest corners of the ISF's self-defined territories in outer space. There were no planets in the Far Reaches, just independent vessels and merchants who preferred not to deal with ISF trade regulations. "That'll provide the best resources to cover your tracks," he said, pointing to me. He thought for a moment, then, "not to mention *your* tracks," he added, his scaly, claw-tipped finger swinging over to Kelp.

Kelp squawked like a startled bird and slithered under his bench to hide.

Duke Frowl laughed, a gurgling hiss of breath that rattled in his throat. The console before him finally chimed with a pleasant little *ding*. Frowl peered up at the screen as the computer spoke:

"Trip update: you are approximately Fifty-five A-Kays[19] from Border Checkpoint Theta. On your current trajectory, you are estimated to make port in fourteen hours' time." The computer voice was unnaturally chipper, especially considering the grim

---

[19] Standard unit for measuring space travel. The 'A-Kay' or 'A. K.' stands for Astronomical Knot.

reality of lifeboat use. "Remember to preserve food rations for triple the estimated time to port."

"So cheery," the duke snarled, swatting at the console to shut off computer assistance.

I chuckled at him, partly to fill the silence.

The duke's olive grey scales seemed to splotch with golden yellow patches along his neck and the sides of his face. I smiled as I realized he was blushing.

"Excuse me," he said, brushing all manner of sludge from his satin tuxedo lapels. "But they make these damn machines too pleasant!" He produced a handkerchief from an inner coat pocket and cleaned his monocle. "Now, where was I?"

"You were saying you have contacts in the Far Reaches," I offered.

"Ah, yes! And the computer said we were bound for Checkpoint Theta. That works out nicely, I should think."

"Oh," I asked.

"Yes," he said. "Though I can't tell you why. But, but, but," he said, raising a claw, "first, we need to find the biowaste chute."

"Of course," I said gratefully, realizing what I'd forgotten in my initial panic. The sad reality of lifeboats was that not everybody made it. A lifeboat departure assumed disastrous outcomes for the mothership vessel. As such, they were required to have a waste chute for dead bodies and other bodily waste to prevent contamination of the circulated air and other environmental life-support systems.

"Spread out and find it," the duke said, taking charge. "We should dump this body before we get too far from the *Ichthus*." He nodded to Corporal Blake's corpse.

Each of us started at stern. I fanned out and traced the hull of the ship along the starboard side while the duke took the port side. Once I was within two meters of the bow of our lifeboat, I stopped searching. The chute's loading compartment was fixed into the pointed bow itself. The duke walked over to it behind me.

"We should've started our search up here," he chuckled. "All right, you," he said, peering back at Kelp. "Time to earn your salt. Come help us move this." With some difficulty, we hefted the corporal's corpse to the little ship's foredeck. Once there, we sat a moment so that each of us could catch our breath. I glanced up, where a substantially sized moonroof of tinted glass offered me a peaceful view of far-off stars. They cruised by as our little ship charged forth, bearing us to salvation.

The disposal of Corporal Blake was awkward. I hesitated, wondering if any of us should say a few words. A lump of guilt sat heavy on my chest, and I tried not to stare at the startled look that still contorted his lifeless face.

Once he was loaded into the chute head-first, I

paused, reaching for the glowing red 'Jettison' button mounted on the wall before us. "Does anyone want to say a few words," I asked with some difficulty.

"Yarh," Duke Frowl gurgled like only a Fallamon could. "He wanted to leave you behind. I'd have shot him, too. All I can say is *good riddance.*"

That was all the closure he offered, and we didn't speak of it again. I reached for the button.

"Wait," Duke Frowl said haltingly. "Where's your pistol?"

I nodded, understanding his request without more explanation. We needed to be on equal footing for the rest of the journey. Duke Frowl was offering a lot in the way of help. Plus, I realized, the gun was technically a murder weapon.

"You're sure you can do something for him," I asked, nodding to Kelp as I pulled the pistol out of my tunic once more.

"I'm a merchant investor," he explained. "I can have him tucked away in the docks of Smith's Pointe before port authority dispatches a retrieval vessel for the two of us." He grinned with pride.

That was all I needed. Kelp had had enough abuse to last a lifetime, I thought. For whatever reason, the slender Komeopian had struck a chord with me, and I felt partly responsible for how he ventured forth.

I nodded, pulled out my pistol, and set it at the front of the compartment, just above Corporal Blake's head. Then, I pressed the button on the wall, and the cylindrical chute closed, hissing shut as it sealed itself off. Then, an electronic buzzing sound hummed through the floor. My teeth hummed with it.

A final whooshing roar, like a burst of air below us, and the 'Jettison' button blinked green three times. "Hazardous materials successfully released." The button turned red again, the chute opened up, and just like that, my crimes tumbled away into the never-ending reaches of darkest space.

July 9th, A.D. 2299
07:32 IST

Shortly after we disposed of Blake, Kelp started complaining about shoulder pain. After some speculation, we cracked open a compact MedBot kit. Despite no information on Kelp's anatomy, the little MedBot drone was able to identify a hairline fracture in the Komeopian's clavicle. A sling and an inflatable bubble-cast were prescribed, along with some pain killers.

"Please be warned," the MedBot informed us in its lazy, nasally voice, "these pain killers contain medical-grade opioids. Do not administer a second dose."

Kelp greatly enjoyed the medicated part of his trip. While he rested, sprawled out prostrate in a bed belowdecks, the duke and I sat near the bow, enjoying the sight of the stars drifting by swiftly overhead. It was like watching the current sweep by on a vast, lazy river.

"It's good of you to be so willing to help him," I said.

"He helped us survive," the duke said with a firm nod. "I can only imagine the bludgeoning I might have taken from that monstrous king of theirs. You saw how he slayed Graves."

I thought about it a moment, then finally I asked, "What do you know about Kelp's kind?"

"Only what Graves told me," he said with a sigh. "He said that their fearsome looks would startle me… which they certainly did. And he said they were dangerous. Beyond that, I'd wager you learned far more than I did for as long as you were with them. What's your honest opinion of our Kelp? I'm under the impression you trust him?"

"I do," I said, realizing it fully as I felt the words form in my mouth, "but only because he covered for us with Dreadnought."

"That was the big one," Duke Frowl asked.

"Yes… the one who took Graves."

"I saw how Kelp was treated by his own species. He was meek, and he was put upon. They had a pecking order, and he was at the very bottom of it."

"This is why you should not let Blake's fate bother you. *He* was selective about who to save. You were not. You are a good person." The duke smiled at me. "I know lesser beings who would have taken this lifeboat for themselves." He winked. "Perhaps that's why you feel responsible for Blake's death… Yes," he nodded, "I think that's it. But that was an accident, my dear lady.

He put himself in that position."

"I still pulled the trigger."

"You were *scared*. I don't think you'd have done it if we hadn't had that surprise attack…" He trailed off, leaving room for me to comment, but I said nothing. The more I thought about everything, the more I felt tears pushing their way up past my cheeks, threatening to spill out all over my face. I felt my lower lip quiver a bit. "Here's the thing," the duke said softly, "I think I would have done the same exact thing in your shoes. I jumped sky-high when that beast came back for us!"

"Thank you," I said sincerely. "That does help to hear."

He nodded, his ovular green head bobbing with enthusiasm. "Now, when we make port, you know mum's the word, don't you? There'll be no more talk of pistols, or Kelp, or Corporal Blake. Otherwise, they'll keep us detained for a fortnight while they interrogate us all to figure out what happened. And if I'm detained, I can't help your harmless little friend."

I nodded. He had no idea how Komeopians reproduced. While I felt bad for keeping it from him, I knew it was just easier to take Frowl's advice and stay quiet. I could understand Komeopian parasitic reproduction being a proprietary secret Graves would have kept from a wealthy passenger. It didn't say much about *Red Dwarf Starliners* valuing the passenger's overall safety. It was such a complex issue that made my head hurt. I had no desire to say more on the matter if I could avoid it.

"As for you, Ms. Galikor," the duke said, raising his scaly, hooded eyebrow, "Let's just say I think you're the one I need to keep an eye on."

"Are you saying you don't trust me," I teased. Despite my playful tone, I was struck with a bolt of nervousness. What had I done to rouse his suspicions? Perhaps he was waiting for me to confess the truth about the Komeopian life cycle? Before my anxious thoughts could rattle on, he spoke again:

"I *know* I can trust you because I've already seen you fight for fairness. Even when it came to giving up your gun. That's a symbolic move to me, y'know? You gave up your power to keep things even. But I'm keeping an eye on you because you're a survivor, and I should follow your lead if I'm to do the same."

I smiled. It was perhaps the most affirming compliment I'd received in a long while.

"Now, if you'll excuse me," he said, his knobby green knees cracking as he stood up, "I should get some sleep before we're picked up. You could probably use some, too."

"You're not wrong," I reassured him before he disappeared into a private sleeping chamber, "but I want to check on our patient one more time."

Mostly, I thought, I wanted to talk to Kelp about keeping his reproductive details to himself. I had to try a few times to make Kelp come to. He was still feeling the effects of his painkillers, and I worried that perhaps he wouldn't remember my advice, but I gave it anyway.

"Nice Scribe helps Kelp," he said with a nod.

"And Shell, too."

I hesitated. "Say it with me once, just so I know you understand."

"Scribe, Kelp never lay eggs in friend." Before I could protest, he slipped back into a deep slumber. I could not wake him again.

His comment at least gave me some comfort. I stayed with him another moment as I thought through things. Kelp was a meek, abused creature who deserved a second chance. I had done all I could to make that happen, and the duke was going to do more. Beyond that, I was not responsible. I couldn't be, I told myself. In the same way that I wasn't fully responsible for what happened to the corporal.

I breathed such a sigh of relief that it coaxed me to yawn. My nerves felt absolutely shot, and it was only in that deep breath that I realized how tired my aching limbs were. So it was that I finally made my way to a sleeping chamber and shook off some of my fatigue and survivor's guilt...

July 9th, A.D. 2299
15:09 IST

For nearly eight hours, I tossed and turned, my sleep crushed into fragments by the nightmarish visions of my experience. In one, the pistol and the corporal's corpse were towed in somewhere, tangled in space slag, and I was brought in for questioning. In another, Kelp laid his eggs in Duke Frowl's chest, and the resulting offspring charged at me like turtles with the heads of land piranha. They nibbled and ripped at my flesh until finally, I woke up in a cold sweat.

I showered and freshened up while the others slept. I was nursing a strong, bitter black coffee from rations when Barrier Outpost Theta made radio contact with Lifeboat 16. The rest of that day remains a blur in my memory, hazy because I was overstimulated by questions and medical exams as soon as we stepped foot in the barrier outpost.

Duke Frowl had been right, I thought. The more information I gave, the longer the process seemed to take. I imagined what another passenger might say if they'd been aboard *Ichthus* without any inclination that the Komeopians had started a localized coup d'état of the starship. Keep it simple, I urged myself.

So, I stuck to easy observations…

I mentioned the bursts of gushing water from the flood, and how I knew something was wrong. I just said I went to the lifeboats and waited. Sadly, I informed my MedBot, Duke Frowl was the only one to show up. I was very casual with my words. More detail would mean more to compare against the duke's story. After three hours, they were finally satisfied, and I was sent to a recovery chamber for a very comfortable night's sleep.

The next morning, I was awakened in my little white room by the same MedBot. After dressing, I let the MedBot lead me to the outpost hangar, where a cheery young patrol pilot was ready and waiting.

"Unless either of you has unfinished business up in Admin," he said, flashing a smile, "I'm ready for takeoff."

What day was it, I asked myself. Outer space had taken its toll on my ability to judge time. Blinking, I glanced down at my datapad, where the date read: July 10, 2299, 05:52 IST.

A fresh new morning, I thought. Thank goodness. I glanced down to the duke, who peered up at me and gave a sharp nod.

"The sooner we leave, the sooner I'm home," I said.

"You heard the gentlelady," Duke Frowl cackled, "not a moment to waste!"

So, we were off.

And that was that.

Corporal Blake's body was never found, nor was my pistol. I couldn't even ask the duke about Kelp, because our pilot, the affable and mustachioed Kenner Mullig, always seemed to be within earshot. Even with his fast talking and his sleek silver ship, it took us nearly two full days to return to safe harbor in orbit around Cliptorgia. I craved the pull of a planet's gravity again. The walls of my many vessels were blurring together, closing in on me in my sleep. I craved fresh air… craved the warmth of a star on my skin through the protective atmosphere of some verdant, spacious celestial rock. It is only natural.

July 19ᵗʰ, A.D. 2319
10:01 IST

After all the years of fearless travel in my early life, I haven't been back to the Far Reaches since that day. There was no point revisiting the memories that died out there… those parts of me driven to the harsh reality of survival. I tried to go there – spent years in therapy for it.

My doctor would stand on the edge of those murky waters beneath Pappy's hatch, but all she ever saw was darkness. A dark, blank void. Instead, my confessions are here, on the page… the safest and truest boundary between which to exchange sentient thoughts and conundrums.

Many years have had to pass, but I can finally revisit that awful experience to recant it here for posterity. We all have at least one dark secret… *Starship Ichthus* was mine, but I have grown weary of carrying it.

After all this time, I can't decide what I would have done in Pappy's shoes. He saw creatures in need, being treated unfairly, and he did the best he could for them. I honestly think he wanted to do the right thing. But our plans, they get away from us all too quickly. I felt bad for him: namely, for the way he died… the way Dreadnought mutilated his corpse.

Still, the memory of Pappy's disembodied head will confront my mind and stir a sickness inside me, and I must distract myself with other things…

Occasionally, I find myself wondering about what ever became of Kelp. I hope he found a better life than what he faced among his brethren aboard the *Ichthus*. I wish I knew where he ended up, how he faired in a whole new sector of the galaxy. The idea of his journey fascinated me; it would have made quite the book! To Pappy's credit, I think I would have taught Kelp the classics of Cliptorgian culture had I been given the chance to share them.

All I shared with Kelp was an awful secret: the truth of our survival… the death of Corporal Blake. I had never taken a life until that final day, nor have I since. I certainly never wanted to, either.

I have tried to forget it… to hold onto the reason and wisdom in the duke's final private conversation with me. But I can't quite see it his way, because of where my guilt truly lies. See, when I remember the shock on Corporal Blake's face, I am merely numb with regret. But when I remember the pain on Dreadnought's dangerously prickly visage in his moments of pain, there's a sinking sadness in the pit of my stomach. I wonder what would have become of Dreadnought had he survived that day. He caused such pain and suffering, and yet, it was easy to see how he was a sad victim of his circumstances.

Lately, I've been forced to look back more and more as recent months have brought about rumors of *Ichthus*'s reappearance in the Outer Rim. The stories seem to leak more and more, like the walls of that damnable starship. They say the ship is of Terran design… that it looks abandoned upon approach… that the engines are dead silent. They say that those who go aboard don't ever come out alive.

I'm afraid I can't tell who the heroes or the villains are in this one. They killed so many innocent passengers, but I cannot say how many of them were killed first. When I remember Dreadnought, I see the beast's misguided inner child… the wounded animal… and my heart feels… sorrow. I pity that brutish being. I glimpsed the miserable condition of his existence, and my soul aches knowing how his whole shiver was treated. Had they been greeted with open arms by our corner of civilization, I doubt very much they'd have been so brutal. Make of that what you will.

ORIGIN OF THE STORY

On June 25, 2005, a group of theater kids in southwestern Pennsylvania set out to make a ten-minute short sci-fi spoof video. In their backyards and basements. Upon seeing the raw footage, it was settled. "We should try to make a series of these over the summer," they agreed. "Like, ten episodes?" Author Brent Winzek, who planned to study filmmaking, had invested in a MiniDV handicam only weeks earlier, making this first cinematic experiment possible. So, the Space Cadets were born that fateful Saturday, after a crew call to sort theater equipment for the upcoming school year.

Over the remainder of 2005, the project introduced Argylesox and Alaborap, Glygorg and the Goliathon, and accomplished their ten-episode goal (plus bonus features). Winzek spent the fall saving money to build a computer for editing down the three-plus hours of footage captured on mini-DV tapes. That goal was realized on December 16th, 2005.

On that same cold winter night, the teenage film crew began filming their first scenes for *Space Cadets Season 2*, the story that would evolve into *Space Cadets and the Legend of the Goliathon*. It was during Season 2 filming that Keptapus, the first Komeopian, was devised from extra costume pieces: a bipedal fish alien who made funny mouth sounds…

The *Space Cadets* underground video series continued producing content independently around Pittsburgh until 2009, garnering enough local attention to produce a live performance, DVDs and other merchandise, and three 'seasons' of the show, each with a premiere screening hosted at local venues around their hometown.

In 2011, Winzek borrowed the Komeopian species from his *Space Cadets* universe to develop a science fiction playscript. Inspired by the first few scenes of Eugene O'Neill's *The Hairy Ape,* the play's goal was to subject a human audience to the 'experience' of an alien mutiny, wherein the theater's audience would serve as passenger seating aboard a luxury spaceship. Throughout the play, the angry Komeopians hurled insults and contradictions at humans, disagreed on how to run their mutiny, and clashed with actors planted in the audience who would represent human passengers and philosophies.

After a workshop table read in 2012, the script for *Mutiny* was revised, but never formally produced. The story collected dust while Winzek focused on other artistic endeavors. From 2014 to 2019, he was working with friend & collaborator Jordan Stine to adapt the *Space Cadets* screenplays into a professionally produced audio drama. It was during pre-production of Space Cadets Radio Season 2: *Space Cadets and the Pirates of the Outer Rim* that Winzek snuck Keptapus the Komeopian back into the universe. It was Stine who asked, "Didn't you write a play about these guys?"

"Yeah," Winzek said. "I should revisit that."

"You should put it back where it belongs," Stine suggested, raising a mischievous eyebrow.

"Where's that?"

Stine grinned, tapping his script. "In the *Space Cadets* universe."

After discussing the new concept as it would fit into the drastically evolved *Space Cadets* universe, it was only natural to bring in story collaborator and *Titanic* aficionado C.J. Barrett. He is the one who first invented the story's hero, Telfera Galikor. Though unwittingly, Barrett also predicted the story's final form when he first produced a character introduction written out in first-person prose.

Finally, after years of fussing, here is the final iteration of that haunting tale about the *Mutiny Aboard the Starship Ichthus*.

ABOUT THE AUTHOR

Author & entertainer Brent Winzek was born and raised in the hills of Pittsburgh, Pennsylvania, where, at age 17, he created the *Space Cadets* universe with the help of his quirkiest, most intelligent theater friends. He attained a Bachelor of Arts in Film Production and a Master of Arts in Theater from Bowling Green State University in Ohio, where he further developed the *Space Cadets* with collaborator Jordan Stine. The project continued evolving in New York City while Brent was working in various circles of the entertainment industry. He continues to write & produce strange original work from deep within a forested hovel with his wife and critters.

To explore other projects, visit
spacecadetsstudios.com

ABOUT THE CO-AUTHOR

Co-author & linguistics master C.J. Barrett was born and raised in Toledo, Ohio on the banks of the Maumee River, where he still resides. He attained a Bachelor of Arts in Theater as well as a Bachelor of German Language Skills from Bowling Green State University in Ohio, where he first encountered a collaborator and fellow thespian in Winzek. Barrett has continued his involvement with Space Cadets Studios through table reads, script workshops, and performances. Mr. Barrett is an artist of many mediums; when he's not writing, he enjoys crafting games, composing music, and painting miniatures.